# A LOVER'S BEAUTY
# THE RAMSEYS
# BOOK VI

## BY
## ALTONYA WASHINGTON

iUniverse, Inc.
New York   Bloomington

# A LOVER'S BEAUTY
# THE RAMSEYS BOOK VI

*iUniverse books may be ordered through booksellers or by contacting:*

*iUniverse*
*1663 Liberty Drive*
*Bloomington, IN 47403*
*www.iuniverse.com*
*1-800-Authors (1-800-288-4677)*

*ISBN: 978-1-4401-1926-2 (pbk)*
*ISBN: 978-1-4401-1927-9 (ebk)*

*Printed in the United States of America*

*iUniverse rev. date:01/20/2009*

# THE RAMSEYS

## Quentin Ramsey
## Marcella Whitman Ramsey

| **Westin Ramsey** | **Georgia Ramsey** | **Marcus Ramsey** | **Houston Ramsey** | **Damon Ramsey** | **Carmen Ramsey** |
|---|---|---|---|---|---|
| (Son) | (Daughter) | (Son) | (Son) | (Son) | (Daughter) |
| *Briselle Deas Ramsey* (Westin's Wife) | *Felix Cade* (Ex-Husband) | *Josephine Simon Ramsey* (Marc's Wife) | *Daphne Monfrey Ramsey* (Houston's Wife) | *Catrina Jeffries Ramsey* (Damon's Wife) | Unmarried |

| *Sybilla Ramsey* | *Sabra Ramsey* | *Moses Ramsey* | *Taurus Ramsey* | *Quest Ramsey* | *Sabella Ramsey* |
|---|---|---|---|---|---|
| Westin & Briselle's Daughter | Felix & Georgia's Daughter | Marcus & Josephine's Son | Houston & Daphne's Son | Damon & Catrina's Son | Carmen's Daughter |
| | | *Johari Frazier* (Moses' Fiancée) | *{Nile Becquois}* | *Michaela Sellars* (Quest's Wife) | |
| | | *Fernando Ramsey* Marcus & Josephine's Son | *Dena Ramsey* Houston & Daphne's Daughter | *Quaysar Ramsey* Damon & Catrina's Son | |
| | | *Contessa Warren* (Fernando's Fiancée) | *{Carlos McPherson}* | *Tykira Lowery* (Quaysar's Wife) | |
| | | *Yohan Ramsey* Marcus & Josephine's Son | | | |
| | | *Melina Dan Ramsey* (Yohan's Wife) | | | |

To the Ramsey fans; new and not so new. Thanks so very much for enjoying the ride!

**She was darkness and light intertwined....**

"I don't even know your name," He pointed out while trailing his fingers across her temple.

Her stare searched his in wonder that she was even there with him. She couldn't resist reaching out to bury her fingers in the thick luxury of his hair. "My name…is that so important?" she asked.

He leaned closer to kiss her mouth. In some way, he wanted to capture the beauty of her words laced in the heavily erotic tone of French. "We've been in bed together for the last two days. I'd say it's important."

She snuggled deeper into the large decadent bed where she lay beneath him. "What would you name me?" She teased, linking her arms about his neck.

For a time, Taurus Ramsey was speechless while taking in the flawless onyx skin, eyes and hair belonging to the woman he held. She was darkness and light intertwined.

"Beauty," He told her simply, his heart thudding with a juvenile intensity when she arched in to kiss him eagerly.

# FIRST PROLOGUE

*Paris, France 1994~*

Eighteen year old Nile Becquois stood at the gate hoping to summon just a faint misting in her eyes. Tears were a hopeless wish, but her mother seemed to need some sort of emotional display to ease her quiet-her shame over bustling her only daughter off to family-strangers actually-in the States.

How could one summon tears when glee threatened to burst the heart? Nile wondered, ordering her mouth not to curve into a smile. Her father certainly had no qualms about her leaving, she thought and the faint smile vanished easily. She remembered the way her mother Yvonne practically had to beg the man just to ride along from their home in Nice to the airport. Cufi Muhammad seemed as thrilled to see her leave as Nile was to be leaving.

Once Yvonne was done speaking with an airline employee at the gate, Nile had at least managed to put a regretful expression in place.

"Oh honey, don't be down. You're going to have the best time." Yvonne Wilson told her daughter and smoothed her hands along Nile's arms in a gesture of assurance. "You're going to see such marvelous things in California."

"I know Maman," Nile whispered, her husky voice laced with the rich accent of her native tongue.

Yvonne looked down, pressing her lips together. "Baby please try not to hate me for sending you away from the only home you know."

"I don't hate you Maman," Nile said, allowing just a faint curve to soften her mouth as she looked down at the woman. Her words were true. She didn't hate Yvonne-not for this. There were far too many other things she had to despise her for. At any rate, Nile saw that her soft admission stoked

Yvonne's tears. She was thankful the job of crying had been taken from her shoulders.

"And I don't want you to blame your father for this," Yvonne urged through a sniffle.

"Please don't speak his name to me," Nile urged as well. Her voice was cold in its softness.

Yvonne nodded, marveling silently at how very different Nile was-so cold, so removed… "We're gonna shut it down baby." She said.

Nile couldn't resist rolling her eyes. "*I* tried to shut it down. I went to the authorities and told them everything about what was going on out there and it's *still* going on which tells me they're in it too-in it to the hilt. Nothing's going to change because the people with the power to change it have far too much to lose. This is why you're really sending me away."

"No baby, no. You're safer this way. It's over baby, I promise you." Yvonne continued to lie.

Nile was drained of her arguments and admitted that her mother was as corrupt as her father and everyone else mixed up in the entire sordid scheme. She recognized her mother's lies about as easily as she recognized the sun rising. Still, she let herself latch on to the tiniest shrivel of hope that it could happen-that in the lie there could be some shred of truth. She let herself believe that the people who had raised her weren't complete monsters. After all, what would that make her?

The intercom voice called out then announcing the flight first in French and then in English.

"Flight 716 now boarding for Los Angeles, California at gate fifteen. Flight 716 now boarding…"

Yvonne stood on the toes of her navy platform pumps and hugged her daughter. "I'll call Aunt Reesy and make sure all went well. You can tell me all about your first airplane ride."

Nile managed a smile though her pitch stare gave away nothing. Satisfied that her mother was done fawning, she hefted the strap of the carry-on bag across her shoulder.

Yvonne watched the young woman blend in with the rest of the boarders making their way toward the gate. She blinked as a steady steam of tears blurred her eyes. When Nile disappeared from view, Yvonne dashed away the tears and look up at the terminal's high ceilings. "Dear God forgive me. Forgive me again."

# SECOND PROLOGUE

### Becici, Montenegro-13 years later~

"I don't even know your name," He pointed out while trailing his fingers across her temple.

Her stare searched his in wonder that she was even there with him. She couldn't resist reaching out to bury her fingers in the thick luxury of his silky crop of hair. "My name…is that so important?" she asked.

He leaned closer to kiss her mouth. In some way, he wanted to capture the beauty of her words laced in the heavily erotic tone of French. "We've been in bed together for the last two days. I'd say it's important."

She snuggled deeper into the large decadent bed where she lay beneath him. "What would you name me?" She teased, linking her arms about his neck.

For a time, Taurus Ramsey was speechless while taking in the flawless onyx skin, eyes and hair belonging to the woman he held. She was darkness and light intertwined.

"Beauty," He told her simply, his heart thudding with a juvenile intensity when she arched in to kiss him eagerly.

"And what would you name *me*?" He asked, once their kiss ended.

"Beauty," Nile Becquois answered without hesitation. Her gaze was undeniably flattering in the manner that it wandered across his caramel and cream complexion as her fingertips savored the silk on satin feel of his skin.

Taurus nuzzled her neck. "I want to keep you," he spoke into her skin.

"Keep me." She repeated.

"I don't want to share you." He clarified, raising his head to fix her with the almost frightening intensity of his champagne gaze.

Nile's quick smile sparked the dimples on either side of her mouth. "You don't even know me. I could be a married woman enjoying a fling. What of my husband?" she teased.

"Leave him."

Nile wanted to laugh, but couldn't. "It would never work. Who I am… who I am would ruin us."

*Couldn't he say the same?* Taurus asked himself. The answer came swiftly. *Yes. Yes he most certainly could.*

"When do you leave?" He asked instead.

"A week," Nile trailed both hands down the hard smoothness of his sculpted chest.

Taurus lowered his forehead to her shoulder, feeling his simmering arousal return to its fully heated state. "Then we shouldn't waste any of it with talk," he decided.

# CHAPTER ONE

*Seattle, Washington-1 year later~*

The beautiful penthouse office at Ramsey Group was bathed in silence. In one of the majestic corner domains, five men sat in stone-faced silence and listened to the revelations shared by the sixth. Once he'd finished, the silence had more to do with devastation than politeness.

"Jesus," Yohan breathed, and moved from his spot on one of the large arm chairs. Easing his free hand into the side pocket of his gray trousers, he went to stand before the floor to ceiling windows lining his cousins' office.

"I second that," Fernando muttered then, stroking his rough jaw as he processed what his cousin had just told them. "Are you sure?" he asked.

Taurus' announcement that his parents had been murdered to 'persuade' them to put all their resources into finding those card keys, seemed so outrageous. But what; they all acknowledged, hadn't been outrageous in their family?

"And how do we know his daughter has them?"

"We don't." Taurus told Yohan. He could have passed for calm had it not been for the muscle jumping along his jaw that belied it all. "Unfortunately, it's all we have as a starting place just now."

"Well did Gray give you anything else to go on?" Quay asked, referring to City Councilman Grayman Sessions who was knee-deep in the affair.

Taurus only shook his head.

"I think we should do it." Moses spoke up then.

Fernando turned to stare down his older brother. "You mean give in to these sons of bitches?" he asked.

1

"Damn right," Moses whispered, leaning forward to brace his elbows on his knees. "Hell, if what T says is true and Houston and Daphne were murdered what do you think those fools will do to the rest of our family?"

Each man's thoughts were riveted on the women in their lives.

Quest left his chair then. He massaged his left arm which now ached in its tell-tale fashion beneath the mocha shirt he wore. Silently enraged, his eyes had gone from their haunting gray to the murderous black. He took root before the windows as well and stared out at the skyline.

More silence loomed and was broken by the sound of Quay slamming a fist to his palm. "To hell with it," he growled, "I agree with Mo but handing over some innocent girl puts a bad taste in my mouth."

"Who says she's innocent?" Taurus muttered and then forced himself to shake off the notion.

"Who says we have to hand her over?" Quest spoke up at last.

"What'cha got in mind Q?" Moses asked.

Quest shrugged, turning to lean against the window pane. "I agree with Moses too. We should find Cufi's daughter, see what she knows. See if she's *innocent*," he remarked sending a meaningful glance toward Taurus. "We'll see if she has those cards. Then we find out how much the damn things are really worth."

Fernando and Quaysar burst into laughter.

"Blackmail brotha?" Quay teased his twin. "Didn't know you had it in you?"

Quest bowed his head in acknowledgement. "So far everyone believes Aunt Daphne killed Houston and herself. We need to keep it that way." He determined, but looked to Taurus and awaited his consent.

"And we keep this among ourselves," he added when Taurus nodded. Every other man in the room spoke up with their own words of agreement.

♦   ♦   ♦

### Los Angeles, California

That afternoon, Nile Becquois was fighting mad. She slammed down the phone receiver and ran shaking fingers across her glossy jet hair.

A stunning honey-gold blonde sat across from Nile and tried not to smile. "Told you so," Darby Ellis remarked.

"Son of a bitch," Nile raged, though her voice never raised higher than a whisper. In a further show of anger, she hurled a slew of art brushes across the floor. It was no surprise that her nerves were in a bunch. That was a usual reaction to a conversation with Perry Finch owner of the warehouse that had been home to her art clinic for the past five years.

Unlike before however, Perry was talking eviction that time. That only meant he'd found another pigeon to scam unspeakable amounts of cash from for the drafty, leaky dwelling.

"Yeah…" Nile conceded, leaning back in her black cushiony desk chair. "He's probably got a new lease already drawn up for his new tenants. He wouldn't budge on that price."

"Because he knows you can't raise it." Darby said.

Nile massaged her eyes and smiled. "Don't you mean because he knows I *won't* raise it?"

"I didn't say that." Darby's voice held an underlying tension below its sweet tone.

Nile rolled her eyes. "You may as well have," she snapped turning her rage on the woman who had been her manager and best friend for over eight years.

Darby gave a flip wave of her hand and stood. "But I didn't," she reciprocated. "This is *your* hang-up," she accused before realizing she'd done so. "I'm sorry Ny," she groaned and let her eyes drift shut.

Fiddling with the oversized cuff of her white cotton blouse, Nile uttered a brief laugh. "Hell, you're right."

"Shit," Darby hissed, coming to kneel beside her best friend's chair. "You're scaring me lately. Why won't you talk to me?"

Nile tried to smile away the question, but couldn't quite manage it. Darby knew nothing of her past-her *true* past. She certainly had no idea about the identity of her scandalous parents. Nile believed she had to keep it that way if she expected to keep her best friend.

"Look I'm sorry," Darby was apologizing before Nile could comment. "I didn't mean to pry," she stood and pressed her hands to her jean clad thighs. "Well…actually I *did* mean to pry but…I just never understand why you have all this aversion to selling your work."

Nile reared back in her chair when Darby went to stand before the bay windows lining the studio warehouse. "Aversion is such a sick word." She finally ground out.

"It's just the way you act whenever you sell a painting-sick." Darby countered, folding her arms over the black cap-sleeved T-shirt she wore. "Is it so bad earning twenty-five to two hundred K plus for a painting?"

"It is when you feel like a whore for doing it. I know-" she raised her hand before Darby could rebut, "another hang-up."

Unfortunately, it was a sad truth that Nile feared would take residence in her soul until the day she died. The apple never fell far from the tree she thought and fiddled with the collar of her blouse. If the sexual nature of her paintings were any evidence, she harbored the same addictions as her father.

She supposed she should be grateful those addictions were soothed in the form of paintings instead of more destructive exploits.

"How in the name of-" Darby stopped herself from snapping, sighed and summoned a calmer tone of voice. "How can you link selling art to selling sex? Okay, okay…bad comparison." She conceded with a grin in light of the nature of the work in question. "I just wish you'd talk to me." She urged silently acknowledging that she was whistling Dixie judging from the resigned look her friend put in place. Stiffening, she slapped her hands to her sides and headed for the door.

Nile's despair warred with her desire to speak up. Despair won.

"You know," Darby spoke over her shoulder as she walked. "I used to think it was funny-you moaning over the fact that the majority of your clients were male. Now I'm beginning to see how deep this goes for you." She turned then. "You won't talk about it, so I can't offer you support here. Not anymore Nile. All I care about right now are those kids. They deserve a place to escape the horror they have to live with every day. They deserve beauty in their lives."

Nile's alluring stare snapped to her friend's face when she heard the sentence. Darby didn't notice.

"They deserve beauty," she repeated, "and if you have to get in bed with the devil to give it to them then you best get past those delicate sensitivities of yours and do it." Without another word, she left Nile alone in the studio.

◆　　◆　　◆

Michaela Ramsey tugged her bottom lip between her teeth when her searching came to an end. She'd been looking all over for Taurus who'd left the sitting room of his parent's home following the reading of their wills.

"Hey? Hiding?" she called out, smoothing a hand along the side of the chic black coat dress she wore. It took some time before her eyes adjusted to the dim lighting of Houston Ramsey's study, but she finally locked in on Taurus sitting there inside. Mick heard his low, grunted response and took that as confirmation that he was indeed hiding.

"House still packed?" He asked once Mick had shut the door and was heading into the room.

She sighed and put a refreshing smile in place. "You know how it is with wills," she teased lightly.

"Like a damned reunion out there," Taurus hissed, leaving the massive white leather chair he'd occupied.

Mick perched on the arm of the chair and watched him venture towards the lighted marble bar which offered the only illumination in the room. "How many have you had?" she inquired softly.

"Four." He answered in a fake, perky tone and tilted his glass in her direction. "I hate drinking alone so join me."

"I can't hang." Mick drawled with a laugh. "One's my limit."

"Alright. One it is."

"How about we talk instead?"

"About what Mick?" he challenged, his hypnotic voice laced with a bit more than its usual edge. "If you came with more condolences, save 'em- you know how I felt about the man."

He was tense enough to snap, Mick thought studying the breadth of his shoulders beneath the worsted material of his black suit coat. "You lost Daphne too," she reminded him in a small tone.

Taurus crumpled then at the sound of his mother's name. The glass he held hit the bar top with a loud clatter.

Mick moved off the arm of the chair with apologies on her lips. Taurus raised his hand to stop her from coming closer.

"She's dead because of him," he grated, his voice growing raspier with each word uttered. "Her life was hell because of him. God why didn't I get her out of here?" he drew a hand through the unruly mass of his hair. "She would've done it. She would've left long before all that came out. She knew he was garbage."

Mick folded her arms at her waist. "But he was still your father." She said.

"And with everything in me I wish I could forget that." He raged and began to pace the study. With a flick of one wrist, a framed portrait of Houston Ramsey was torn from the wall and stomped beneath the bottom of his son's loafer.

"I think you're trying to do more than forget. I think you're trying to understand and you're angry because he can't help you do that."

"And how the hell could he do that Mick? How could he *help* me? He couldn't help me if he were alive and well and sitting in that fucking ridiculous chair!"

"Do you remember what you told me about going to see Houston in jail?" Mick asked, venturing closer while clutching her hands. "About how he looked almost genuine- truly remorseful…and then he told everything he knew- almost like he was honestly trying to maybe atone for it all." Mick watched Taurus as he leaned against the wall and slowly raised his cool champagne stare to her face. "Now he's gone," she continued, "and you'll never know if he really meant it. If he was really capable of changing."

"What the hell difference does it make Mick?" He whispered with a shrug and pushed off the wall to take a seat on one of the noisy gray leather sofas. Grimacing at the sound, he opted to stand instead. "What does it matter?" He repeated.

Mick moved before him then. "It matters because you're afraid that whatever was inside Houston is inside you and you need to know if *he* could change because you need to know if *you* could."

The words hit home and sent the rest of the bottled emotions spewing. Taurus crumpled for a second time and leaned down to rest his head on Mick's shoulder as he accepted her hug.

"I'm scared Mick," he admitted after they'd embraced for a long time.

"You'll never be like him. You're too good for that." She swore while smoothing her hand across his back. "Inside you're good-at the core and that's more powerful than anything you think you may've inherited from your father."

With a grunt, Taurus pulled away. "If I'm so good, why am I still alone then, huh Mick?"

The question threw her so that she was speechless. She honestly had no clue the man even had those kinds of hopes.

Taurus grinned, his eyes narrowing in amused fascination that he'd stunned her. "Well?" He challenged, savoring the moment.

"Well I...um..." Michaela could never recall being as robbed of the ability to speak as she was then. "Well," she restated with a shrug and put a little distance between them. "The uh right one usually comes along when you're not looking. Isn't that what they say?"

"Ah...so you weren't looking when my cousin came along?"

Mick's amber gaze warmed over in the dreamy fashion that was usual when her husband was mentioned. "No..." she sighed, lashes fluttering at the thought of Quest Ramsey. "All of a sudden he was...he was just there and he wasn't going anywhere."

"And now you guys are the happiest couple I know- complete with your own little doll."

Mick smiled again, thinking of her beautiful six month old baby girl then. "Quincee's my life," she breathed and looked back at Taurus then. "That's why I know where you're coming from with all this." Taking a seat on one of the noisy sofas, she leaned forward and allowed her curls to tumble into her face. "I was so stressed when I found out I was pregnant. More than anything, I wanted to know where my mother was. I only wanted to know if she'd changed or if she was the same heartless bitch who left an eight year old child to raise herself."

Forgetting his own agitations, Taurus joined Mick on the sofa and pressed a hard kiss to the top of her head.

"See I was terrified that the same...evil was inside me- if I could ever leave my child like that," Mick confessed, her light eyes glistening with sudden tears.

Taurus nodded, rubbing a lock of her hair between his thumb and forefinger. "How'd you get past it?" He asked.

Mick looked down at the furry white carpeting beneath her pumps. "I just realized that I already loved Quinn more than my life and that's a helluva lot more powerful than wondering about the motives of a woman who's pretty much dead to me." She shook her head. "I'd find no 'words of wisdom' there- so I had to move past it." She shared and hoped she sounded convincing enough.

"Like I need to," Taurus guessed and smiled his agreement. "I s'pose it'd be a lot easier to do if I had what you do-family."

"Taurus you-"

"No Mick. My *own* family." He corrected mimicking her position on the sofa by bracing his elbows on his knees. "I'm terrified that I'll never have what my cousins have all been lucky enough to find. I think about what my father did," He massaged his thumb into his palm and focused on the gesture, "I wonder if I should even *think* about family when there's the possibility that I could put a woman through that."

Mick clutched his wrist. "You couldn't do that. To anyone."

"I did it to Zara."

Michaela stiffened, recognizing the name of the woman who had affected so many of the Ramsey men. "What happened to Zara was Marc's fault. The sooner you accept that-"

"Her getting pregnant and being told to get rid of it-that was *my* doing not my uncle's. All that happened with Zara made me realize how much I wanted that life-that family. To prove I could be a better man than Houston-that I could love unconditionally."

"And you can, but finding the *right* woman won't be easy-especially for you."

Taurus bowed his head. The muscle jumping along his jaw was a tell-tale sign that he was working feverishly to keep his emotions in check. Still, he'd come to depend on Mick for honesty and she never failed him no matter how bittersweet the truth was.

Mick had cast her eyes upon the floor, knowing he meant for her to go on. Hell, she shouldn't have been surprised to see that her comment had stunned him.

Taurus Ramsey had the ability to only speak to a woman and have her ready to bear his children-Mick had heard countless women say it since she'd known him. She was sure it was a gift envied by many men. But what man wouldn't envy the power Taurus and his cousins held over the opposite sex?

Beautiful was what women called Taurus Ramsey and even that accolade seemed sub-par. At six foot four and leanly muscular, his complexion compared easily to a milky shade of coffee. The skin was flawless, the eyes a remarkable champagne color-truly unsettling in their intensity. Yet when he spoke, a woman's eyes fell to his sensually curved mouth.

"You're too beautiful." Mick said, punctuating the softly simple remark with a shrug. She took in the face framed by the mass of heavy curls that often grew unruly and had once dared to brush his shoulders. It was usually tamed-somewhat-into a more acceptable cut but even that couldn't pull the eyes away from the unexpected shade of light brown with natural streaks of a darker brown visible throughout.

Taurus rolled his eyes and muttered a vicious obscenity as he stood. The man viewed his so called "beauty" as more of a curse than a blessing. He now believed that while women may crave a night-several nights-in his bed, few were interested in anything more involved.

"You're the kind of man women read about in romance novels, drool over on soap operas. A man she never intends to meet-never really wants to-not on a daily basis. You're…a fantasy-something to be put on a shelf and taken down for pleasure only. I know that's not who you are." Mick interjected when he faced her with fire in his gaze.

"But I think it's what most of the women you see know you as." She smirked. "In their defense, I think it's all you let them see because of this fear you have of being like Houston."

Taurus knew it was true. How often had he exploited his numerous physical and mental assets which drew women in droves? With those women he could pretend he was everything good about the Ramseys-looks, power, respect. The entire package. With *those* women he could forget the secrets, deceptions, crimes…

"Hell Mick, so what?" He snapped, not wanting to acknowledge that particular truth. "Does that mean I'll never have what you and Quest, Quay and Ty and everybody else has been blessed to find?"

"No honey, it means you'll have to wait for the woman who wants you more than the fantasy." Mick explained, turning to face him more fully from her position on the sofa. "You'll have to wait for the woman you'll allow to see beyond that fantasy to the vulnerable less than perfect but just as beautiful thing beneath."

Taurus drew a hand through his hair and looked as if he understood exactly where Mick was coming from.

"How will I know who she is?"

Mick leaned back on the sofa and folded her arms over her chest. "My guess is you won't. Not until you stop looking for her and not until she becomes as desperate to be seen for her true self as you are."

# *CHAPTER TWO*

The woman Michaela Ramsey described to her husband's cousin was; at that very moment, placing a tentative knock upon the office door of her business manager.

"It's open!" Darby's high-pitched melodic tone tripped through the light oak.

Nile couldn't stop the brief smile that tugged at her mouth. That sweet tone Darby possessed could turn firm and demanding in a flat second. Twisting the knob, Nile entered and stood just inside Darby's cheery office.

Darby stood behind her desk once she saw Nile. They watched each other for several moments standing in silence until they both cried "I'm sorry!" in unison. Laughing, the two friends met in the center of the office.

"Did I ever tell you my big fear?" Darby asked watching Nile frown a bit even as she smiled and shook her head. "I've always wanted to find my father's family and," she paused to squeeze Nile's hands, "I don't know…make a connection-trace my roots…" she shrugged and closed her eyes. "My fear is that they'll take one look at my blonde hair, green eyes and *brown* skin and call me trash…or worse."

Nile stepped closer to her friend. "Darb-"

"Let me finish Ny, please." She sighed, eyes still closed. "Anyway, it makes me feel like a disgusting coward and keeps me from doing something so simple. It's stupid."

"Mmm…like your fear of storms?" Nile teased, smiling when the comment had the desired affect and Darby smiled. "It's not stupid," Nile argued, her tone firming a bit. She was well aware that Darby's bi-racial status had caused her more than a few uneasy moments.

"Well I think it is." Darby countered with a shrug. "It's probably why I gave you such a rough time before. Sometimes the simplest things can be the hardest to handle if they trigger some fear you try your best to ignore."

She gave a saucy wink. "We'll find a way to save this place. I'm with you no matter what."

Nile hugged Darby then and pulled away. "Why don't you tell me about your plan to sell enough canvas to save us?"

Darby cocked her head. "You sure girl?"

Nile nodded. "No," she admitted with a shaky laugh. "But this is for the kids and I'd walk through hell for them."

Darby searched Nile's face and apparently believed what she saw, for she smiled. "Well this is gonna be sheer heaven and we won't have to *plan* a thing."

"How does *that* work?"

"Hotel Brillante wants you back for another event."

"Brillante," Nile breathed recognizing the name of the Montenegro hotel. She listened as Darby told her how pleased the hotel owners were with the showing she'd done the previous year. As Darby spoke, Nile let her thoughts drift back to other events that occurred during the trip. Events that included a sinfully beautiful man and two days spent making love in his bed.

"Ny? You alright girl?" Darby asked, having noticed her friend's far away expression and the soft moan she uttered.

Nile nodded. "When do we leave?"

"The show's set *tentative* for next Saturday night." Darby carefully announced before cocking her head again. "You really okay with this Ny?"

"Confirm the date woman!" Nile ordered and joined in when Darby laughed. While Darby clicked over to her desk to arrange the details, Nile excused herself. Outside the office, she leaned against the closed door and caught her breath. It had happened over a year ago and still the images of him were as vivid as they were on the day she'd left him asleep in his suite. Shaking her head, she ordered herself to focus on the situation. Saving the studio-her kid's safe haven-had to be her top priority.

Smiling then, Nile glanced back at the door when Darby's happy laughter lilted through it. Darby Ellis was a good friend with a beautiful heart. She could be making obscene amounts of money handling PR for some high powered politician or celebrity for her compassion and beauty radiated outward on any and everything she touched.

In spite of that, Darby had suffered most often because of that very beauty which had the power to achieve such wonderful successes. Nile understood for she too experienced much of the same. Staring across the hall, she caught a glimpse of her reflection in the mirrored framing surrounding one of her portraits on the wall outside the office.

Men always stared her way as if they couldn't believe what they were seeing. It didn't faze Nile for she'd understood the nature of men at an early age and realized their staring was simply in momentary fascination over something they'd never seen before.

In spite of Nile's 'aversion' to the tug of looks, she was a beauty. Huge dark eyes tilted alluringly and rivaled the flawless dark of her onyx skin tone. The small nose and double dimples drew attention to the lush curve of her mouth. Despite her stunning height, she'd stubbornly always sought to blend in-which she could never do. The amazement she glimpsed in men's eyes only made her feel more like a circus freak instead of some incredible beauty.

Nile could only see the negatives. She felt her boobs were too small and decided that was good-one less thing for men to gawk at. Her hair was a glossy straight jet black that she could recall the women (and girls) in her father's employ constantly pulling to test its authenticity. Nile usually wore the tresses hanging long to shield her face unless she was with Darby or…her mother.

Of course her attempts to *blend in* and go unnoticed were moot once she spoke. The low husky voice laced in the unmistakable erotic of French could grab attention from across a room. The sound could keep a listener captivated by her every word.

Her work was the only thing more erotic. It had been praised by the best, but Nile knew it was her 'beauty' that brought in the bucks. Her buyers were almost exclusively male-no surprise there given the seductive quality of her paintings.

For Nile, unfortunately there was nothing else. She hoped that by drawing until her hands cramped, that she'd one day be rid of the visions that drove her motivation. Selling the work made her feel dirty-too similar to her father. Cufi Muhammad had made his sleazy fortune dealing in sex and Nile swore to never be like him. Yet there she was creating work that depicted images which sold because of that intriguing line they drew between erotica and pornography. She hated herself and what drove her talent even more. All her life she'd seen women's beauty be used against them. She'd seen them abused because of it.

She didn't want to be beautiful because beauty destroyed and could be destroyed. Of course, if her work or her beauty had the power to save her kid's oasis, she'd damn well use both to the best of her ability.

♦   ♦   ♦

Mick was leaving the study after her talk with Taurus who wanted more time alone. She was turning from the closed door and a smile brightened her face when she saw yet another Ramsey heading towards her.

Sabella Ramsey leaned down to kiss her cousin-in-law's cheek. "Girl thanks so much for putting me and mama up with you, Quest and the baby."

"Hush." Mick whispered with a wave of her hand. "You knew we wouldn't think of having you two stay in a hotel when we've got all that room. So how *is* Miss Carmen? I haven't had time to chat with her much since you guys got here."

Sabella's lovely face brightened with a smile which seemed more content than humor-filled. "Better every day," she sighed, her almond brown gaze settling on her mother across the room with Damon and Catrina. "I can't figure out why she's so... jubilant lately, but I'm not about to complain."

Mick slapped her hands to her sides and grinned. "I think everyone's happier with Marc gone."

Sabella turned back to Mick. "You think?" She asked, her slanting stare narrowing further.

"He's escaped," Mick reminded her in a matter-of-fact tone, "he's...a wanted man and that alone is repugnant enough to keep him out of Seattle. I'll bet with any luck the man isn't even in the country. Hopefully he'll keep it that way."

"Yeah...hopefully," Sabella agreed and then shook her head as if she'd remembered what she'd found Mick for. "Have you seen T? Dena's looking for him."

"Yeah he's in the study," Mick waved a hand across her shoulder, "we were just talking-"

"My Lord Michaela, you've been at Taurus's side more today than your own husband's."

Mick's expression took on a humorous glean when she rolled her eyes and turned to face Georgia Ramsey the second eldest child of Quentin and Marcella Ramsey. The woman had never approved of her nephew marrying an ex-reporter with no proper roots. Mick would never tell the overbearing woman how much delight she took in bringing her down a few pegs.

Georgia stood looking down at Michaela. Her back was as straight as the grim line of her mouth. "I wouldn't expect you to know how inappropriate it is to flit between two men that way. Especially when one is your husband." She studied the diamond bracelet that seemed to accentuate the gray silk of her blouse. "You've been practically hovering over Taurus all afternoon."

"Aunt Georgie..." Sabella warned.

"No Belle, it's fine," Mick assured before crossing her arms over her chest. "I guess we're just two of a kind George and me." She drawled, smiling wider when Georgia winced over that particular shortening of her name. "You've been *hovering* over Miss Carmen all weekend-not to mention butting into conversations that don't include you." Mick tapped a finger to her chin as though she were concentrating. "Or are you-are you trying to ignore the fact that no one really wants to talk to you George?"

Thoroughly exasperated and embarrassed, Georgia clenched her fists and stomped off. Sabella didn't bother to smother her laughter.

Mick shook her head, watching Georgia stomp all the way out of the spacious sitting room. "Give my apologies to Sabra for talking to her mom that way."

"Are you kidding?" Sabella cried, blinking tears of laughter from her lashes. "My cousin's gonna hate herself for missing that!"

"You should remember we're at the reading of a will-a somber occasion." Johari Frazier murmured, her lashes fluttering close as she surrendered to the delightful shrills of sensation stemming from Moses' lips brushing her jaw.

Moses fiddled with the row of buttons lining the back of Johari's dark dress. "You being here is the only thing getting me through this," he growled and inhaled the cocoa-mango fragrance clinging to her skin. "Family gatherings have never been my thing."

"Well I'm happy to help," Jo crooned, linking her arms about his neck. "I'm also happy that you're having a change of thought regarding your family. They really need you now."

Moses grimaced knowing Jo was referring to the death of Houston and Daphne as well as Marc's disappearance. He, of course, knew it went far deeper than a shoulder to cry on.

Jo tilted her head and noted the sharpening of his striking dark features. "Ram?" She whispered, tugging on the knot of his black tie.

His sharp features grew sharper still with the onset of male desire. "Call me that again and I take you home," he threatened, drawing her into a kiss.

"Mmm…Moses," she just managed to whisper during the kiss. "Baby you're vibrating."

"Damn right."

Laughing, Johari angled out of his embrace and managed to push him off. "It's probably your phone."

Muttering a curse, when he realized their kiss had reached its end, Moses pulled the cell from his side trouser pocket. "Yeah? Yeah Linc, what's up?" He greeted Lincoln Cooper one of his detectives at Ramsey Bounty. While Lincoln gave his report, Moses only absently listened. He pulled Johari close again and focused on nibbling her earlobe and drawing her obscenely close as that nibbling gained intensity.

"What?" He hissed into the pencil-slim phone.

Johari's heart rushed to her throat as she leaned back to watch him.

"Say that again...no, the name." Moses ordered. "No, no I got it. Thanks. Thanks Linc, I'll be in touch."

"What is it?" Jo asked once he'd put away the phone.

"Jesus," Moses whispered, smoothing a hand across his jaw while his mind raced.

"Moses?"

Wincing, he pressed a quick kiss to her cheek. "Nothing. Business. It's nothing." *Or everything*, he acknowledged in silence. "We need to go." He decided. The look on his face and tone of voice brooked no argument.

♦    ♦    ♦

Dena Ramsey was on her way to the study in search of her brother. She found Carlos McPherson instead. She was speechless, having not seen the man; she once thought she'd marry, in over ten years.

"I'm sorry," he said and closed a bit more of the distance separating them.

It was several seconds before she locked in on what he meant. "Thank-thank you," she managed as the sorrow re-asserted itself. Greedily, her dark eyes feasted on his handsome face. Then, catching herself she rolled her eyes and tried to move past him.

Carlos wouldn't allow it and simply blocked her way with his imposing frame. He was just as greedy to stare at her-absorbing every aspect he'd missed after all the years.

"How are you?"

Dena bowed her head and savored the sound of his voice. "T and I are on our way out of town." She said mostly to let Carlos know that she wouldn't be around for any of the many detailed conversations they could surely use.

He didn't seem to care and simply moved closer. Clearly he wanted to do much more than look at her.

Every part of her ached to have him touch her. She resisted. "Please," she breathed.

"Why?" He challenged.

"You know why," she countered, snapping out of the spell he'd cast so quickly.

Carlos didn't try to stop her when she brushed past him. "No Dee," he watched her race down the hall, "no but it's damn time I found out."

♦    ♦    ♦

Taurus decided to confirm airport transpo to the Hotel Brillante before he left the study. When the call ended, he replaced the receiver and stood before the desk with his head bowed. God, when Dena told him she wanted to take him to Montenegro, he almost collapsed. If just the name stirred such a reaction, he'd surely collapse once they got there.

Of course, Taurus knew it was more than just a name. It was a woman-the dark beauty he'd met and who wasn't out of his system even after a year. He'd cursed and criticized himself for much of that year for not following his own desires and at least pressing her more about her name. Just some hint and he'd have found her. Still, he remembered the fear in her eyes when he tried to uncover more. She was hiding yet it was unclear from what or who. He knew he'd give anything to know and protect her from it.

He'd accepted her need for anonymity because he was just as wary of telling her who he was and witnessing the shock and disgust in her eyes when she recognized the name Ramsey. He'd accepted her plea for anonymity because what they'd enjoyed over the course of that week-not to mention the two days spent in his bed-had been worth it. More than worth it. There was a part of him that still yearned to hear his name on her mouth. If fate smiled upon him once more and gave him another chance with her, he'd fill that desire. Whatever it took.

Shaking away the cluttering thoughts, Taurus tuned into Moses calling him.

"T? You alright, man?" Moses patted Taurus' shoulder when he nodded.

"Gangin' up on me?" Taurus asked when he noticed Fernando walking into the study.

"Got a call from one of my detectives," Moses headed to the bar for a drink. "We may have a lead on the daughter-nothing concrete yet though. I know you need to go with Dena so I asked Fern to come along."

"D will understand if I cancel out."

Moses was already shaking his head. "She's suffering man. She needs this-needs to get away."

"But not without the proper escort in light of the dangers now lurking." Fernando cautioned.

"You need time away too," Moses noted while Fernando nodded his agreement. "You're still ragged over what happened to Aunt Daphne-don't try to deny that man."

Taurus wouldn't put on airs for his cousins. "You let me know the second you find somethin'," he told them.

"You got it." Moses agreed and then joined Fernando in giving Taurus a tight hug.

# CHAPTER THREE

"You wanna slow up on those?" Taurus asked without opening his eyes. He'd overheard his sister across the cabin of the jet as she whispered a dainty 'thank you' to the flight attendant. Then, there was the barely audible clink as she exchanged an empty glass for a full one.

"Just settling my nerves," Dena said and sipped at her gin and tonic. "You know I don't like flying."

Finally Taurus opened his eyes and twisted the black swivel he occupied. "Who are you tryin' to fool?" He asked, fixing her with his unnerving light stare.

"You know I don't like flying." Dena reiterated while frowning at the taste of the drink. "Even if we are on a *Ramsey* jet," She pointed out and set aside her glass.

Taurus leaned his head back against the chair. "You should've thought of that before thinking of this trip idea."

Dena smiled, knowing he was goading her to keep her mind off her woes. "You're gonna kiss me when I tell you my surprise."

"I thought the trip *was* the surprise?"

"Part of it."

"Lord help me." Taurus sighed and began to massage his eyes. "If you love me, you'll spare me from the waiting."

Dena toyed with a lock of her wavy shoulder length hair and shrugged. "Stop being so dramatic," she drawled and decided to give in when he glared her way. "Remember back when I came out for Quest and Mick's wedding? We had lunch one day in your office and I noticed all the artwork and complimented on how incredible it made the place look?" She smiled and tugged on the cuff of her plum blouse. "Your assistant Minyon told me most of the pieces were by the same artist and that you were on a mission to acquire as much as you could. I commented on the uh…raciness of the work and she said you keep the most erotic pieces in your home office."

Taurus was sitting up straight then, his attention riveted on the story. "What are you up to Dee and what the hell does it have to do with my art collection?"

Dena looked out over the never ending sea of clouds past the jet window. "I tried to get more information on the paintings-anything that I could find on them or the artist but there wasn't much luck at first. Then just over a year ago, I found out that there had been of showing at this Hotel Brillante in Montenegro. I called and asked about it but they couldn't give me any specific dates other than telling me the occasion was part of a week long cultural soiree for their guests. So…I asked to be put on the guest list in hopes of being notified should the artist make another showing." Dena cleared her throat as her eyes clouded over with some solemn emotion. "They called last year and told me Nile Becquois was to be there but well…with everything going on…"

Taurus moved to sit next to his sister and they hugged tightly for the longest time.

"Why'd she have to die?" Dena asked, crying softly into the sleeve of her brother's winter blue polo shirt. "Why couldn't she have just killed him?"

"Shh…" Taurus urged, kissing her temple.

"God," Dena moaned and drew back a bit. "I'm sorry. That was a terrible thing to say."

Taurus shook his head. "No need for apologies-not for that."

Silence descended in the elegant cabin and then Dena seemed to order herself out of the mood for she suddenly smiled. "We're gonna have a great time. I guarantee it."

"I believe it," he spoke against her forehead and looked down to find light in her eyes. He felt his own mood improve ten-fold.

◆    ◆    ◆

*Becici, Montenegro~*

Nile ordered her mouth to close lest it hit the plush honey wheat carpeting that covered the grand expanse of the living area. The Hotel Brillante was well deserving of its name for its lavish allure was evident in everything from the stunning lobby to the gold fixtures in its massive bathrooms.

Darby was tipping the bellman and thanking him for placing her bags in her own room. When he left, she turned to see her friend watching her in disbelief.

"What *is* this?" Nile breathed.

Darby didn't pretend to misunderstand. "I booked you an apartment suite," she explained, pulling off the toffee colored cotton jacket she wore.

"I don't need all this." Nile argued, inspecting her surroundings again.

"We'll be here for two weeks-enough time for you to handle your business and enjoy a little pleasure."

"I've had enough pleasure here to last me a lifetime," Nile grumbled.

"Excuse me?"

"I can't use all this Dar." She remarked, running her fingertips along the lattice screens that marked the entrance to the living area. The overstuffed furnishings shrieked comfort and decadence and were only enhanced by the grandness of the stone fireplace. The earth and gold tone color scheme added coziness hard to resist.

"Well you've got two weeks to come up with all kinds of uses," Darby consoled, pulling her card key from the back pocket of her jeans. "The showing's tomorrow night and after that it's fun, fun, fun."

Nile rolled her eyes, but Darby knew her friend appreciated it. Besides, she had a sixth sense that Nile would most certainly benefit from two weeks of being pampered. Darby yawned then watching as Nile drifted further into the apartment. "I'm seriously jet-lagged, gonna turn in," she called already turning to the main door. "Don't wait on me for breakfast I'm sure I won't be up before noon."

Nile watched as Darby strolled out then she continued the tour of her elaborate digs. The breathtaking terrace/balcony was shielded from the room by billowing floor to ceiling drapes. She had a feeling sleep for her would be a long time coming.

◆　　◆　　◆

"They're gonna kick our asses for this, you know?"

Quest Ramsey grinned sparking his left dimple when he slanted a glance toward his cousin. "I've been married to Mick almost three years and bein' kicked in the ass by your wife is somethin' you best get used to cousin."

Fernando rolled his eyes. "Forget it. I already been inducted into that club," he said his thoughts focused on his fiery tempered fiancée just then.

The provocative and soothing rumble of male laughter silenced when the door opened to Quest's office. Michaela walked in followed by Contessa. Leaving their seats, both men greeted their visitors.

"What's this all about Quest?" Mick managed to ask once her husband was done kissing her senseless.

"Thought this would be a good place to talk," he said. Intoxicated by the provocative fragrance clinging to her skin, he took a few extra moments to nuzzle his favorite spot behind her ear.

Mick wanted to say more, but scandalous tingles stabbed her relentlessly and her only thought was *God he's good at this…*

Contessa still had a bit more of her verbal ability left however. "What do we need to talk about? Ramsey?" She called when silence met her question. The next sound she uttered resembled a moan as Fernando suckled her earlobe while his thumb circled a firming nipple beneath the cotton fabric of her antique peach wrap blouse. Biting her lip, County decided her answer could wait.

In unison, Quest and Fernando left Mick and County standing where they were. The cousins resumed their seats in the office. Fernando waved a hand to Quest.

"The release of '*Royal Ramsey*' is to be postponed until further notice." He announced.

Mouths forming perfect Os, the women exchanged glances stunned that Quest and Fernando even knew the title which had only been agreed upon a few months prior during a private teleconference with the Chicago office.

"Spivey's dead." County breathed, knowing the leak had come from her Senior Editor Spivey Freeman. "What Ramsey? Did you remind him that you saved my life and that he owed you?"

Fernando grinned. "I didn't have to. Spivey is a reasonable man and understands that sometimes things have to be done for one's own good."

"Even when *one* is an adult and the damn publisher and *owner* of the company?" County seethed.

Fernando inspected a tiny imperfection along the sole of the tanned Lugs he sported. "We didn't have to come to you with this, you know?"

"The hell you didn't!"

In the midst of Fernando and County's sparring match, Quest could feel Mick's amber gaze boring holes into the side of his head. Finally he met her scathing glare.

"We don't want to get legal with you both." Quest coolly threatened his wife. "Whether we'd be successful is irrelevant. We can tie that book up in so much red tape it'd be a century before it hit the shelves." He broke eye contact with Michaela then, knowing she was seconds away from jumping across his desk.

The cousins nodded at one another and stood.

"I'm um…gonna head out to meet Mo at the airport," Fernando hastily decided and figured it'd be best not to kiss his fiancée goodbye.

Quest took a different route. Casually slipping a hand into the pocket of his pine trousers, he crossed to his wife. He leaned down and kissed her slow and deliberately before patting her hip and leaving behind his cousin.

The office was bathed in silence once more.

♦ ♦ ♦

## *Becici, Montenegro~*

Taurus and Dena adjourned to their respective rooms upon arrival at Hotel Brillante the previous evening. The siblings fell into their beds where both swore not to leave for at least ten hours. With adjoining suites, it was easier for Taurus to overhear his sister crying out early the next morning.

Leaving his own bed and making his way through the pre-dawn light, Taurus pulled open the adjoining door in time to see his sister thrashing amidst the bed covers. Muttering a curse, he raced over to pull Dena into his arms.

"Hey, hey, shh...Dee? Shh...babe it's me, it's me Taurus. Shh... it's alright, it's alright..."

It took some doing, but eventually the woman's eerie jerking and moaning slowed. Her eyes were blurred by tears when she finally opened them and looked at her brother.

"Better?" Taurus asked, kissing Dena's forehead when she barely nodded. "I wondered how long it'd be before you had another," he mused, feeling her stiffen against him.

Dena raised her head and allowed him to see her confusion.

"You only have the really bad ones when Carlos McPherson's on your mind." He clarified and kept a tight grip on her when she would've pulled away.

"You're wrong." She pouted.

"I disagree," he argued and loosened his hold after a moment. "I put it together after seeing him at the funeral and then the will reading."

Dena rolled her eyes. "He was only there for a minute to talk to Moses about something that couldn't wait."

"Mmm...yet he made sure his quick visit included time for him to speak to you."

She replied with a short laugh. "And how would you know when you were holed up in dad's study for most of the afternoon."

Taurus shrugged. "Aunt Georgie told me."

The name of their father's older sister stoked laughter as it often did and the mood lightened immediately.

"Are you gonna tell me what the dream was about?" Taurus asked, toying with the baby hair smattered at Dena's temple.

She shook her head. "It doesn't matter anymore."

Taurus however, could see that it mattered very much. Her eyes held the haunted quality they'd carried since Houston Ramsey was arrested for Sera Black's death. Still, he decided to let it alone for a while.

"You up for breakfast?" he asked instead.

"I'm starved," Dena admitted and her features began to brighten. "Can't wait to try one of the hotel's five-star restaurants."

Taurus kissed her cheek. "You got thirty minutes to get ready."

"Hold on," Dena laughed, "some of us need more time to make ourselves beautiful. Forty-five minutes and you got a deal."

"Done."

Dena slapped his cheek playfully and left the bed for the bathroom.

Taurus rested back in his sister's bed. His expression was pensive as unsettled thoughts re-cluttered his mind.

♦    ♦    ♦

## Ketchikan, Alaska~

Melina Ramsey smiled and snuggled back into her husband's massive frame. Following the horrific loss of her cousin Zara, Melina found herself blessed by being remarried. Yohan spared no effort or expense to indulge his wife. He hoped the time away would help her to deal with the grief. He believed his job had been accomplished when the weeks spent at their lovely Alaskan cabin helped to melt away his wife's sadness.

"Knowing Zara's gone-really gone is a million times better than wondering what's become of her." Melina admitted one dusky evening while she and Yohan enjoyed the extraordinary view from their bed. Smiling, she turned on her side to face her husband. "I'm ready to go home."

Yohan's striking dark face tensed with concern. "You sure?" he queried, watching the serene yet firm smile slowly curving her mouth. "We can stay here forever if you like."

Melina leaned close to press a soft kiss to his jaw. She knew he meant every word and loved him even more. "I'm sure Han. I feel better than I have in so long and I know I have *you* to thank." She smoothed the back of her hand across his sleek chest. "Besides, it's time I get back to work." She said, thinking of all that had probably accumulated on her desk at Charm Galleries during the brief time they'd been at the cabin.

Yohan was frowning. "Why do you sound so happy about it?"

"Because I am. I think maybe I'll organize a few showings when I get back." Nodding over the idea, Mel turned on her back and focused her sights upon the incredible view. "I've got a life to live and I think Zara would've wanted me to get busy livin' it." She decided smiling when Yohan kissed her forehead. After a while however, a somber expression clouded her face. "I'm still so angry Han. I don't know if anything will ever take that away."

Yohan understood. "Because of Marcus," he guessed.

"I'm sorry." She whispered for causing him to think of the man. "I just feel sick when I think about him escaping and basking on a beach somewhere."

Yohan toyed with the stitched edge of the sheet that was covering Melina's breasts. "Would you feel better if I told you I don't think the man's basking?"

Mel turned to face her husband again. "But he escaped Han. Indulging in pleasure to celebrate that is something I'm sure he'd have no problem doing."

Yohan sat up then and braced his arms across raised knees. "Something just doesn't feel right about it all."

"What doesn't feel right?" Mel asked, noting the stiff set of his back then.

Yohan massaged the back of his neck and shrugged. "The hell if I know. Besides Ma, I've got nothing else to go on."

Melina pushed herself up to sit as well. "What's Josephine got to do with it?"

"She's too calm. In my opinion she should be hoppin' mad." He said, the ocean depth of his voice adopting a dangerous intensity. "She shot the jackass Mel. Wanting him dead and knowing he's traipsing around livin' the life has to eat at her. In spite of it all, I know she's got no problem voicing displeasure-least not to her sons," he acknowledged with a lazy grin.

Melina contemplated the observation as well. "You know it *could* be as simple as her finally accepting things for what they are. Deciding to get on with her life, you know?"

Yohan wasn't nearly convinced, but urged himself to shrug it off. He bumped Mel's shoulder with his own before pulling her close. "You're probably right." He said.

◆    ◆    ◆

Nile decided to take Darby's advice and enjoy the elaborate offerings of the Hotel Brillante. In all her travels, the hotel had always stood out in her mind as the most exquisite destination she'd had the delight of enjoying. The grand, spacious establishment sat along the glorious seemingly untouched waters of the Adriatic Sea. Mesmerizing gardens decorated every entrance from the lush dining rooms and lounges to the apartment sized suites and hedonistic spas. Every desire could be imagined or realized. Enchanting beaches, towering mountains, canyons and forests offered the entire country of Montenegro an allure like few others. Nile was determined to pamper herself from head to toe.

Feeling wonderfully optimistic as she headed into the Oval Dining Room for breakfast, Nile decided to take the call that had her cell phone vibrating. The sight of Yvonne Wilson's name on the face plate was usually cause enough to let voice mail intervene. But since she was living optimistically, participating in a conversation seemed like a good place to start proving it.

"Le Bonne Maman de Matin," she greeted her mother good morning while passing the restaurant's gated entrance.

"More tea for the lady, Sir?"

Taurus smiled while shaking his head. "No need Daunte, she left for the spa already."

"Very well. Anything else for you then, Sir?" The young waiter inquired.

Taurus debated, taking a second or two in order to scan the seductive beauty of the lush garden past the balcony where he and Dena had enjoyed breakfast. Beyond the sea of vivid flowers and brush was an equally vivid sea of blue.

"What the hell," he sighed and chose to stay a while longer. "Bring me two more of those stuffed crepes, will you Daunte? And is there any more of that berry coffee?"

Daunte grinned. "The last cup is yours, Sir. I can have the kitchen put on another pot if you'd like?"

"Don't go to the trouble Daunte, thanks." Taurus nodded when the waiter went to see to the order.

Taurus indulged in enjoying the view once more. There was a chill in the air, but he savored the breeze. The wind tousled his hair and the material of the black shirt he wore outside sagging khaki trousers. His attention on the landscape, he missed the lingering stares and obvious plays for just a glance or two. One woman was bold enough to stop right next to his table and *absently* mention her stockings being twisted. Of course, she had to raise her skirt obscenely high to properly observe the sheer hose. Realizing that she'd gone unnoticed by Taurus, a pout curved her lips seconds before she flounced off.

Daunte returning with his order was the only thing that drew Taurus' attention from the sea view. After thanking the waiter, he dived right into the second hearty portion of strawberry and cream cheese-filled crepes. He'd been eating heartily for almost eight minutes when he glanced up and almost choked. In the midst of a swallow, Taurus found himself looking upon the woman he thought he'd never see again.

"Je serai beau. Je n'ai pas besoin de tout cela. Maman…."

It was her alright, Taurus thought-as if he'd ever come close to seeing anyone who even remotely resembled her. Still, even if a case of mistaken identity was the issue, no one could mimic the voice. The husky lacing of French-erotic and beckoning had haunted his dreams for well over a year.

"Oui…oui Maman…Au revoir," Nile ended the call and then hefted the slender phone in her palm. She was torn between shoving the cell back into the trouser pocket hidden beneath her beige cashmere wrap and tossing it into the Adriatic. She opted for the former and decided to see if food might soothe her simmering temper.

The fact that her mother had called out of concern for her safety would have been laughable had Nile not known the real motivation behind Yvonne's *interest* in her well-being. Those damn card keys had to be behind the root of it all. During the past months, Nile had come to realize how very important they were. She'd connected the names and faces to several powerful players in the business and political world.

If she knew her father-and she did, the man was most likely debating and hoping to use the keys for some sort of financial gain. Those small cards could be a powerful tool for blackmail. Her every instinct told her to take them to the police and let the chips fall.

The question was her mother. Yvonne's *concern* had to be for the cards and Nile's intention for them. Of course, Nile knew her mother as well as her father. The woman's plan wasn't to assist her husband, but to outwit him. Were her plans for blackmail or something more evolved? It was a question Nile believed she'd never find an answer to. One thing was clear though: she held the keys-literally- to her parent's survival or ruin.

"Miss Becquois?"

With a start, Nile saw the waiter watching her curiously. Taking note of the pad he held, she cleared her throat and casually withdrew a menu from the table she stood next to. She closed it the moment she opened it.

"I think I'll take breakfast in my room. Could you have the service send up two stuffed crepes-peaches and cream and a pot of that berry coffee?"

Daunte nodded while briskly noting the order. "The kitchen will need to brew a fresh pot of the berry blend. Your order may be just a moment longer."

Nile's smile was polite, but brief. "That's fine." She breathed and whisked past him.

Taurus sat leaning back in his chair. Eating was forgotten and he appeared as though someone was holding his throat in a vice. Struggling to breathe, he watched her leave the balcony with the hem of her wrap floating gracefully about her.

"Daunte?" he just managed to call out when the man approached his table. "The um-the woman you were just talking to…"

Daunte chuckled after a moment, understanding Taurus' reaction. "Quite a vision, yes?"

24

"Yes…she's staying here?"

"Yes sir, Mademoiselle Becquois has returned to grace us with another show."

"Becquois?"

"Nile Becquois," Daunte clarified, taking time to give the phonetic pronunciation 'Beck-wa' before he continued. "Her art shows always draw the largest crowds with the deepest pockets if you'll excuse me for saying, sir."

"Thanks Daunte," Taurus stood then and dropped several bills to the table before pushing more at Daunte. "Thanks," he repeated and left the balcony without another word.

# CHAPTER FOUR

Nile decided she'd made enough of an effort at getting out and about for the day. She contemplated visiting the spa later and felt it best to keep her cell off for the duration of the trip. She'd quickly exchanged the stunning wrap, pantsuit and boots for a pair of slippers and a lounging robe. It was back to bed following breakfast.

She glanced at the living room clock when the bell sounded. Moving fast, she whisked open the door for room service and found herself leaning against the door for support upon realizing who waited in the hall.

"Mademoiselle Becquois," Taurus greeted in a sly matter-of-fact tone.

The sound of his voice sent her stumbling backward on the thick slippers she wore. All the while, she tried to ignore the raging tingles that would soon lead to a wealth of moisture soaking her panties. She had never forgotten his voice-heavy and sweet with a surge of roughness. The sound reminded her of Caske and Crème rippling over chipped ice. Having it touch her ears in reality was a guaranteed path to orgasm.

Several moments passed before Nile realized she'd been backing away from him as he advanced slowly. Clearly he knew he'd stunned her stupid but was undeterred in his decision to advance nonetheless.

"Wait," she barely uttered. Clearing her throat she tried again only nothing came of the effort that time.

Taurus was in as much shock as Nile. She was even more incredible standing before him than she'd been in his dreams. She was elusive and lovely, alluring yet with a blatant innocence of which she seemed completely oblivious. He swore to himself that he only wanted to touch her-to prove to himself that she was real. Then he'd go-honestly he would.

"Please," she managed on a gasp when she saw his long strides grow bolder. Reflexively, she extended her hand to stay him.

In one fluid move, Taurus caught her wrist. Unfortunately, it was just as the backs of her knees touched the edge of the monstrous sofa filling a corner of the living room. She tumbled back and he followed, knocking the wind from her chest when he landed on top of her.

Sure enough, the raging tingles stirred a flood of liquid need inside her panties. Her lashes fluttered and she caught her lip between her teeth. The gesture drowned whatever remained of Taurus' restraint. He dipped his head and thrust a hungry tongue deep inside her mouth. The kiss effectively smothered the surprised and wanton groan that rose in her throat.

Nile responded with an eager impatience and arched herself to silently urge his attention past her mouth. He took the hint, moving on to feast upon her throat in the same hungry manner that he'd taken her mouth. His hands cupped her breasts, simultaneously stroking the firming nipples beneath the fuzzy pink material of her robe. They were instantly ready for his tongue when he tugged the robe from her body.

*What are you doing?* Nile heard the words ring in her head and promptly ignored them. There were far more delightful things to focus on just then.

Taurus' thoughts ran along the same lines as he sought to dismiss all logic from his mind. He'd pretty much invited himself into her room and proceeded to force himself on her. He'd heard the 'wait' on her lips and knew her reaching out to him wasn't an invitation, but he couldn't think. Until he had her-had all of her, he couldn't think.

Nile covered his hands on her breasts with every intention of tugging them away. Useless. Taurus massaged them with more determination until satisfied by the way her nipples firmed against his palms. He raised his head to pleasure himself with the look of her.

She kept her eyes closed, fearing that if she looked upon his face, all reasons of why they shouldn't be involved in…this would scream out at her.

Working one nipple between his thumb and forefinger, Taurus trapped the other between his lips and teeth. Just barely, he raked the rigid tip. His tongue scarcely outlined the nub and a surge of arrogant confidence swelled inside him when her whimper reached his ears.

Having been denied his touch for over a year, Nile could take no more of the maddening foreplay. Her hips ground upon his and she hissed that he please her in the fashion they both needed.

Taurus had grown tired of the sweet interlude as well. His mouth suckled madly upon her breast and alternated ever so steadily between his perfect teeth. His free hand fisted around a wad of the lounging robe causing the loose belt to unravel at Nile's waist and reveal the rest of her dark figure.

Nile wanted to lose her fingers in his gorgeous light hair but had no strength for anything except the frantic arching of her hips against his. Taurus wasted no more time. He continued the savage suckling on her breasts while tugging away her underwear and then freeing himself from the confines of his trousers.

Nile felt her heart thundering at the base of her throat when he parted her thighs and settled between. An instant later, he was sinking deep inside her. What remained of her breath caught on a weak cry while she savored his throbbing stiff length buried in a wealth of her need.

Taurus shuddered, resting his head on her shoulder in order to relish her tight heat housing him. For every thrust he subjected her to, desire seemed to ache anew. The pleasure of taking her was an equal dose of torture and elation.

His movements began to slow after what seemed a delicious eternity. Yet when Nile's responsive cries grew more helpless and affected, his desire intensified yet again and his thrusts gained strength. The lounging robe she'd worn was a wrinkled heap about her. Nile refused to imagine what a scandalous picture she made, giving herself so eagerly to the fully clothed man above-a man whose name she still didn't know.

♦    ♦    ♦

"That's it. That's it. Keep 'em open."

Nile couldn't even muster enough strength to frown at Darby; whose instructions were delivered with just a bit too much perkiness. Her lashes fluttered close and Darby's voice lost its perk and gathered steam. It was then that Nile understood 'keep 'em open' must've been in reference to her eyes.

"What are you doing?" She managed once her eyes were opened to slits once more.

Darby tapped an index finger to her chin and pretended to concentrate. "Let's see…I think I'm trying to wake you up."

"Smart ass," Nile grumbled. "I was only taking a nap," she explained while trying to sit up.

"And I'm pleased to see you resting but you've got little over an hour left before the show."

"What?" Nile hissed hair whipping round her face as she looked past Darby to the dark skies beyond the open drapes. "An hour? But-but I was about to have breakfast."

Darby laughed; her honey blonde curls bobbing as she nodded toward the untouched cart of food waiting at the foot of the bed. "I wondered about that, but things fell into place when I read the card." Her eyes narrowed devilishly. "Then, of course, there's the fact that you're naked."

"What card?" Nile blinked, purposefully ignoring her best friend's inquisitive stare and the fact that she was indeed naked in the tangled king bed. "What card?" She repeated, grimacing when Darby went to retrieve what she'd found on the room service table.

Strolling toward the bed, Darby scanned the card again and decided to read aloud. "Thank you- Taurus Ramsey."

Whatever sluggishness Nile had been feeling was dashed away like dust being cleared by a bucket of cold water.

"Ra-Ramsey?" She breathed, wondering and praying it was just a coincidence. Surely he wasn't one of *the* Ramseys. All she wanted then was to sink back into bed.

"*Thank you?*" Darby drawled not noticing Nile's reaction as she was too busy teasing her. "He leaves you breakfast and in bed for an entire day. Need I ask what you did to deserve such thanks?"

"Darby...don't."

Tilting her head then, Darby strolled close and folded her arms across the front of the sunflower yellow top she wore. Taking note of her friend's strained appearance, she knelt beside the bed and squeezed Nile's hand. "Is everything okay Ny? Did this guy... do anything?"

Nile hesitated but a moment before answering. "Well...he did *many* things."

Darby grinned. "Apparently. Were they things *you* wanted-is what I mean."

"God yes," Nile responded without hesitation that time, but uttered a weak curse just the same. "I shouldn't have."

Darby tugged on a lock of Nile's hair. "That's what we usually think about one night-or in your case-one *day* stands."

"I know him." Nile shared, smiling at the surprise on Darby's face. "This wasn't our first time."

"Alright what the hell's going on?"

"It's a *very* long story."

"How long?"

"About a year."

"I'll take the condensed version," Darby decided and then raised a brow. "But I'll expect the uncut story when we're done with everything. So get your ass in the shower and start talkin'.'"

◆ ◆ ◆

"Does Johari know you cry when you get pissy drunk?" Fernando watched his brother slosh an eighth helping of Hennessey into the stubby beaded glass he held.

Moses grinned but it fell short of reaching his eyes. "No." He told his brother.

Fernando tilted back the rest of his Bourbon-helping number six for him. "Well just make sure you don't ever let her see you this way. You're a pitiful sight when you're like this. You don't want her to turn tail and run now that you've finally got her."

Now Moses' laughter came through full and rich. "She's seen me at my worst. I think she can handle it."

Fernando massaged his eyes. "Yeah…folks can handle all sorts of shit if you give 'em a chance."

Moses' eighth glass of Hennessey vanished like a flash. "I know where you're goin' with this."

"And?"

"And *what* man? Hell…" Moses groaned, smoothing a hand across his bald head. "All I intended to do was conduct a simple investigation-find what we need to get these keys, secure the family's safety and bury this whole mess." He leaned against the desk in Fernando's office and began to smooth suddenly damp palms across his jeans. "Now I've uncovered shit that's another can of poison. Somethin' that could rip a hole through two people we love a lot."

Fernando clapped his brother's shoulder on his way to the bar. "So what are you gonna do?"

"Gotta tell Taurus and then we go from there, I guess." Moses sighed, folding his arms over his chest while he debated. "I'm in no hurry to move fast though. It can wait 'til he gets back from Montenegro. No need to upset his time with Dena."

"And in the meantime?"

Moses stood. "In the meantime, we need to sober up." He headed behind the bar to program the coffee pot for six cups. "And you need to get home to your fiancée." He told Fernando and then smirked. "I was plannin' to propose to Twig after all the funerals and will readings were done," he said using his pet name for Johari. "Losing Zara almost destroyed her. I don't want any more ugliness to touch her."

"Then don't let it." Fernando said, reaching beneath the bar for two coffee mugs. "You've wanted Johari for your wife since forever and waiting for the perfect time is the last thing you need to worry about."

Moses' laughter roared through the office then. "Perfect time in the *Ramsey* family? Brotha you're drunker than I thought!"

Fernando raised his empty Bourbon glass in a mock toast and joined his brother in laughter.

◆　　◆　　◆

Montenegro evenings were even more breathtaking than daylight hours. It was a dreamscape with a maze of lights twinkling in almost every exquisite corner. The light reflected off the serene waters of the Adriatic in a manner that was nothing less than hypnotic.

Amidst its own lush gardens and perfectly groomed lawns, the Hotel Brillante was yet another glittering star amongst the rest. Inside, its guests were dressed for evenings touring the city's nightlife or enjoying all the events going on inside the immaculate hotel.

The biggest draw had to be Nile Becquois' showing. It wasn't that strange for the reclusive artist to appeal to huge crowds which generated hundreds of thousands of dollars for her work. As she rarely held showings, the lofty figures were as much for the quality of the art as they were for the mystique of the artist herself.

Darby could hear Nile's fifth sigh in the quiet confines of the elevator car they shared.

"Think you'll see him tonight?"

"No." Nile managed trying to ignore the lurch in her stomach when she spoke. "Please don't ask such questions if you expect me to get through this evening without making a mad dash back to my room."

Darby waved her hands about her in a gesture of serenity. "Just try to think about the kids. That should keep your feet on the ground."

Nile agreed, her thoughts going right to the twenty kids who sought her studio—*their* studio for solace. God, how often had she wished for a place to escape to when she was a child? Still, in spite of the grossly inappropriate things she'd seen as a child, they didn't hold a candle to what her kids witnessed on a daily basis. Witnessing murders and having their lives endangered while playing outside their homes or *inside* their homes… No, she would not lose that studio. She'd do whatever was needed to ensure that.

The elevator doors opened on the corridor leading to the Hotel's Galleria Brillante. Nile raised her head, checked her chic black gown through the mirror in the car and then exited and greeted her patrons with the grace of a queen.

Taurus decided to keep a low profile for the duration of the evening; which would be easier said than done because of his sister. Dena was determined to fulfill every promise that he'd enjoy himself which including introducing him to his favorite artist. Little did Dena know that nothing could improve on the enjoyment he'd already had. Well…maybe only the opportunity to enjoy it again.

Taurus recalled the day's events while observing his view of the gallery from his seat in the deep black armchair nestled in a far area of the large room. A full year had passed and he feared she'd ruined him for any other. He hadn't even considered the idea of dating-not that the offers were frequent.

It was as Mick said, he was beyond that. He needed more. He needed a woman as desperate to be seen for her true self as he was. Why he thought Nile Becquois was that woman, he had no idea. Perhaps it was the sadness, the unease in her lovely stare that said more than words.

*Or perhaps it was just the need for a healthy dose of sex*, a voice pointed out in his mind. Taurus smiled, tugging on the cuff of his black double-breasted suit coat while acknowledging the truth in that statement. That day in her suite reminded him of their time together a year before. What they couldn't or wouldn't express in words came through in act. She allowed him to possess her and he in turn was possessed. The more he took of her, the more he'd wanted until exhaustion dealt its hand.

Unlike before, he thought, he wouldn't lose her. He wouldn't let her out of his sight until they spoke. Heaven help her if she thought to brush him off again because he didn't think he could allow it without a fight. If it meant fighting dirty…so be it.

"Smart man."

Taurus looked up realizing it was the gentleman standing next to his chair who spoke and not another voice in his head.

"Smart to take a load off and simply wait for a chance to speak with her," said the grinning man who extending his hand for Taurus to shake. "Claude Neveau," he said and stared out over the crowd as well. "Yes, I have a feeling Miss Becquois will be caught in a crowd for quite a while." Turning back to Taurus, Claude waved a hand toward an empty chair. "May I?"

Taurus only dipped his head. "Are you a fan?" He inquired lightly once the gentleman had settled in the chair.

"Who wouldn't be-especially a man?!" Claude playfully scoffed.

Taurus laughed though his striking light gaze remained void of any humor. Leaning back in his chair, his gaze followed Nile across the room while Claude Neveau rambled on.

"…her allure goes far beyond her work-which is genius-erotic genius… she's beautiful and tough, but she's like crystal. You can't see *how* tough until you get close or as close as she'll let you before the steel and cold settle in."

"Hmph, you don't sound bitter over it." Taurus noted.

Claude shrugged. "To have a beauty like that even glance at you is nothing short of heaven. But it's not only her looks." Claude cautioned while making himself more comfortable. "It's the *look* she gives you when you're speaking to her-the look that says she's heard it all before and knows you're full of shit."

Taurus silently urged his hands to uncurl from the fists they were clenched into. "You sound as if you know her well," he inquired of Claude, wondering if the man knew how close he was to having his face disfigured should the answer displease him.

Claude shrugged. "Not as well as I'd like to. In truth, I've only met her during the few shows she puts on every other year or so." He brushed a stream of lint from the hunter green fabric of his tailored suit. "My boss is a huge fan and often sends me to make purchases for his buildings. Still…I hope one day my acquisitions will be enough."

"For?"

Claude grinned. "Well my friend, it's widely known that she dines with whoever buys a painting and has a private dinner with the *top* buyer. Hell, when one canvas can start at twenty-five thousand and go up, I guess she feels it's the least she can do."

Taurus rested his head back against the chair. A soft smirk curved his mouth but he offered no response.

# CHAPTER FIVE

"I have *got* to get something to eat besides these damned canapés."

Darby continued to look over the note cards she'd been using during her speech. "You had a perfectly good meal go to waste in your hotel room because you were… otherwise occupied."

Nile's gaze shifted toward the elaborate updo Darby wore. "How'd you like me to rip out one of those curls?"

"No need to get snippy."

"Then how long are these jokes gonna last?"

"Long time. It ain't every day-or every year for that matter that I get to tear into you over something so steamy."

Nile curved a hand around the knot in front of Darby's crimson halter dress. "Look you tear into me all you want but I have *got* to get some real food."

"The refreshment table is filled with-"

"Let me revise my threat to rip out curls."

"Listen," Darby squeezed Nile's upper arms, "just hold tight for a few more seconds. My announcement should take your mind off your stomach."

"You just become more deluded with age, don't you?" Nile criticized, rolling her eyes in a bored manner when Darby supplied a devilish laugh and sauntered away.

Alone for the first time that evening, Nile had nothing but an empty stomach and a head full of visual images from her morning, noon and afternoon with Taurus Ramsey.

God, he was a Ramsey. One of *the* Ramseys. She knew that without a doubt and could've laughed and cried over her luck. Wondering if he knew who she was-who her father was-set every part of her on edge with worry… and fear. Goosebumps broke out along every part of her bared by the daring cut of her plunging V-neck gown. She was most thankful for the intrusion on her thoughts when a patron tapped her shoulder.

Nile turned to smile down at a petite dark woman with fresh, lovely features and waves of shoulder length hair framing her face.

"Forgive me for scaring you," Dena apologized with a laugh. "You've been surrounded by a crowd for much of the night and I so wanted a chance to speak to you."

"No, it's fine." Nile assured her with a laugh of her own. "Thanks so much for coming out for the show."

Dena's expressive gaze scanned the elaborate room. "I'll bet these things get pretty tiring after a while," she noted.

"You've got no idea," Nile agreed. "It's such a treat talking to a *female* guest for a change."

"I can imagine." Dena fiddled with the flaring sleeves of her navy blouson dress. "I did wonder why there were so many men."

Nile shrugged and looked around the room as well. "The nature of my work is very um…provocative and tends to appeal to more men."

Dena grinned. "Well that explains why my little brother is such a big fan."

"Well that's still always good to hear!" Nile raved.

"Then you'll be pleased to know he's filled his office and home with your work. If he had his way a piece of your work would be on every floor of every Ramsey building."

"Ramsey?" Nile queried, her dark gaze narrowing slightly.

"Oh please forgive my manners," Dena apologized with a laugh and extended her hand. "Dena Ramsey. My brother Taurus is a huge fan and when I heard about your show, I knew I had to get him here."

Nile summoned strength to her weak hand in order to return Dena's shake. Now on top of an empty stomach and explicit images from that day's heated romp, she had a heart racing to block her throat and burst her eardrums.

Thankfully, the lights dimmed just then and everyone's attention was directed towards the stage. Darby stood there beaming and waiting for a modicum of silence before addressing the crowd.

"Good evening! I'd like to thank you all for coming out to partake in this rare treat-a showing by Miss Nile Becquois!"

Applause and whistles followed Darby's opening line.

"Your support of Nile also supports the kids she works daily to provide a place of beauty and hope. But tonight, it seems that one person in particular will obtain all the praise for ensuring Nile's kids maintain their studio. I'm thrilled and honored to announce that this show consisting of all twenty pieces selected from the artist's most private works are the sole purchase of one of our guests here tonight!"

Thunderous applause tore through the hall. Nile's eyes glazed with tears. She joined the rest of her guests in looking around the room in search of the generous patron.

"Now for the bad news," Darby added while waving her hands to regain the crowd's attention. "Tonight's very giving patron chooses to remain anonymous. The canvases will be on display through the end of next weekend, so please enjoy them as well as the delicious refreshments in the rear of the gallery. Thank you."

"Oh congratulations!" Dena remarked and shook hands with Nile again. "I apologize for my brother missing in action, I so wanted him to meet you."

Nile covered Dena's hand with her own. "It's no problem and I won't be leaving for a while yet so I'm sure I'll meet him before then." She lied and hoped the woman couldn't tell.

"Sounds great. I'll let you get back to your guests." Dena said, and shook hands before excusing herself.

Darby was tapping Nile's shoulder a second later. "Still hungry?"

"Don't do that." Nile warned.

"Well your anonymous benefactor is waiting in the Oval Dining Room.

Elated simply by the possibility of a meal, Nile kissed Darby's cheek and set off.

Chuckling, Darby pulled out her cell phone and selected the number she wanted. "Perry, this is Darby Ellis. Get our deeds prepared, we're ready to buy you out."

Nile tried not to appear too eager to chow down when she strolled into the Oval Dining Room. She prayed this anonymous patron wasn't a big talker else they were about to find the dinner conversation truly one-sided; at least until she had a fair amount of food in her belly.

"Mademoiselle Becquois," the lone host greeted and waved Nile past his stand. "You'll be dining with your guest in the enclosed portion of the balcony. It's all arranged."

Nile followed the man and wasn't surprised to find the place deserted with only a setting for two. Person spends almost $300,000 dollars for art; least they can do is arrange a private dining room she thought.

Moreover, *this* private dining room was already stocked with that evening's meal. Nile practically swooned as she took in the modest yet impressive spread of chicken parmesan, various pastas, salads and fruits. She helped herself to several grapes, slices of cantaloupe, cherry tomatoes and celery stalks. Her mouth was full of cucumber spread and cracker when she realized she wasn't alone.

Seeing Taurus Ramsey across the room sent her emptying the champagne glass she held and blindly setting it back upon the buffet.

"You," She ground out while swallowing.

Taurus bowed his head. Hiding both hands in his trouser pockets, he walked forward. "I know you have dinner with whoever buys a painting. What happens for the person who buys it all?"

By now, he was standing right before her and Nile could only blink owlishly for a time before her verbal skills kicked in.

"It uh…it's never happened before so I guess we'll have to play it by ear."

"Right," he agreed with a nod. Keeping both hands in his pockets, he stepped closer and dipped his head intent on kissing her again.

Nile cleared her throat and backed away. "I sure am starved," she mentioned and cleared her throat again.

"I'm sorry," Taurus grinned and knocked his fist along the buffet. "For the way I bulldozed my way into your day."

The smooth clarification sent a wave of dizziness through Nile's head. She pressed the back of her hand against her cheek.

"Here," Taurus whispered taking her elbow and urging her to sit.

Nile obliged, watching as he returned to the buffet where he mentioned something about preparing her plate. "Thanks," she murmured keeping her eyes on him while she tried to tug more material across her breasts bared by the deep V of the gown. "I don't like spinach," she said noticing as he set a portion on her plate.

"It's good for you," he said and added another helping for good measure.

"Why'd you do this?" Nile asked after a few moments of silence. "Buy me out and all? According to your sister you already have several pieces."

Taurus smiled at her mention of Dena. "It was her idea to come here."

"Really?" Nile's surprise was evident and took her right back to the previous year when they'd spent two days in that very hotel.

Taurus was thinking of it as well, but felt it best not to make mention. Things were uncomfortable enough. "I'm sure I won't have a problem finding a wall for each piece," he set a plate before her and then fixed his own.

Nile wasted no time diving into the delicious meal. She'd devoured at least a quarter portion before Taurus took his place at the table.

"Don't flatter yourself." She knew that he was watching interestedly as she wolfed down the food. "I was already starving long before I saw you today."

Silence took its place and the two of them enjoyed the meal. Nile helped herself to a second portion-including the deliciously seasoned steamed spinach.

"So why'd you buy all my paintings?" She asked again once she was stuffed.

Taurus shrugged and finished off the last corner of his chicken parm. "I've always been a fan of your work." He said, absently wiping his hands on the cloth napkin that lay next to his plate. "Dena says I'm obsessed," he shared in a much softer tone.

"Was that before or after you discovered I was a woman?" Nile focused on what remained of her dinner when asking the question.

"Before."

She nodded, her brows rising in slight surprise. "You impress me Mr. Ramsey. Most men won't admit to that."

"Admit to what?"

Nile tapped her nails along the edge of her plate. "To buying such blatant displays of sex and from another man." Her smile was intentionally coy. "My work is often compared to pornography."

Taurus was almost mesmerized by the allure of the words flavored by the sound of her accent. A muscle flexed along his jaw but he was able to remain focused on his meal. "Clearly those who think that aren't able to sway the thousands of folk who buy your work." He reached for another bottle of his preferred Killian's. "You've got critics praising it and they've helped to make you one of the most acclaimed artists in the world-not to mention one of the wealthiest."

Impressed again, Nile's dark gaze narrowed and she raised her glass toward him in toast. "You've certainly done your homework."

He grinned. "*That* was after I discovered you're a woman." He admitted.

Nile let herself enjoy the moment and joined him in laughter until his exquisite stare sharpened. He studied her with an intensity that could have stopped her heart.

Taurus returned his focus to what remained of the food. "Anyway, it was the only way I'd get to see you again, right?"

"And why is that so important when you've already gotten the top prize?"

"Maybe I want more."

"*More?* More of the top prize?"

"More *than* the top prize."

"Why?"

The question stoked Taurus' anger and his knife dropped with a loud clatter upon the stoneware. "Come off it, already. You know what I mean. You knew a year ago that I didn't want you to leave."

Nile shook her head and began to massage the nape of her neck. "We've got no more of a chance at working out now than we did a year ago."

"How do you know?" He challenged his voice taking on a rougher more dangerous undertone.

Nile rolled her eyes and threw down her napkin. "Why didn't you tell me who you were?"

"You wouldn't let me."

"And that's the *only* reason Mr. Ramsey?" She inquired watching his beautiful features tighten into a hard mask. "Clearly your reasons for accepting my not wanting to know your name are still prevalent. Why don't you just let it rest at the fact that we were attracted to each other and decided to enjoy that." She felt restless beneath his unwavering glare and left her seat.

"Why can't you just chalk it up to fantastic sex and let it end Taurus?"

"Because I don't want to."

She laughed. "And you're a man who always gets what he wants?" Heavy sarcasm laced her voice.

"Not always," he admitted while standing. "Usually-not always."

Nile clapped her hands to her sides. "Then can't you just take this as one of those 'not always' times?"

"Why'd you sleep with me?"

Nile was on her way to the door when she heard the question. "I told you." She bowed her head as if defeated.

"Fantastic sex?" He threw back. "That's it? You really buy that?"

Nile whirled around to face him then eager to take the bait. "Why does it sound so strange? Because I'm a woman and women are supposed to attach heartfelt emotion to a man before she sleeps with him? Bullshit."

"And that didn't come into play with us? Not once?" He asked his temper dangerously close to boiling.

"No." She lied, knowing far more than sex had *come into play* during her time spent with him. *So what? You won't have a chance with him once he learns who your father is.*

"You were a quick bit of fun." She spoke slowly, provocatively watching the muscle dance along his jaw. "A sexy diversion during an otherwise boring trip. Sex was what it was. Gratification. *Meaningless* gratification."

Taurus kept quiet though every part of him was raging. Her relaxed stance and the casual way she tapped her foot in the chic heels she wore didn't fool him at all. Every part of him said she was lying, but why did it matter? He wondered.

Of course it was just as she'd said. What they'd shared was gratifying in every sense of the word but he wouldn't accept it as meaningless. Why? Because she was illusive, dark, beautiful with a voice that was the personification of erotic? Yes. Still, there was so much more and he couldn't let her go again until he found out what that was.

Nile took advantage of the silence between them and basically ran from the dining room. When the door closed behind her, she let her tears escape in a flood.

♦    ♦    ♦

## *Los Angeles, California~*

Yvonne Wilson set down the phone with great effort. It was taking everything inside her not to call Nile for the umpteenth time and leave an umpteenth message on her cell. The last thing she wanted was to alienate her daughter. Well…more than she already had.

God, what a mess she'd made of *everything*-so many mistakes and regrets. And now she was in the process of making yet another and for what? To hold onto some part of the elaborate lifestyle she'd come to know and love? Yes, but this time *she'd* call the shots. The money that flowed in would be by *her* doing-*her* way.

She'd hated lying to Nile. Sadly, it'd become a thing she'd learned to do very well. Even sadder was the fact that now her daughter could see the lie forming in her eyes before it even tripped from her tongue.

Whether Nile believed her or not, Yvonne prayed there was enough doubt to keep her from turning over those card keys. She also prayed Cufi didn't find Nile and run some 'you're my last hope' guilt trip on her. Ironically, that seemed to be the case for both she and her dear hubby. Those keys were the tickets to both their salvation. Unfortunately, the pay off couldn't be shared. When the time came, Yvonne knew Cufi would make it a fight that would see one or both of them dead.

♦    ♦    ♦

"You must know all these recent…upsets don't sit well with my family."

Cufi Muhammad managed a chuckle in spite of the very real fist of fear that was curving its way about his innards. "Women aren't hard to replace in this business Gabe, you know that." Somehow he managed to sound cool.

Gabriel Tesano let a few moments of silence precede his words. "No, but when one loses women who were privy to the sort of information they held…you understand our concern?"

"I do." Cufi could almost see the blood lust in Gabriel's eyes despite the fact they were speaking by phone. "Please know that I'm doing everything in my power to recover those keys."

"That's good to know."

Cufi expelled a tiny sigh. "Once I do, it'll be the word of those foolish girls against ours. Without those keys there'll be nothing to link certain members of your family to my organization."

"So you think my concern is the card keys?"

A softness colored Gabriel's voice which could have been considered understanding had Cufi not known the man better.

"You should know that while my father's face graces one of those keys, I'm not overly concerned by them. Not as much as I am by other matters."

Cufi dared not speak then.

"I'm concerned by what those *rescued* young women might share- things that our lovely Ms. Zara tried to share. Locations to a certain island getaway for example."

Cufi dared to laugh. "But everyone believes that's a myth. No one would take any ramblings about it seriously!"

"Well we'd prefer not to take that chance." Gabriel chuckled. "Calm down Chuck, all we need you to do is provide the names of the young women you lost."

"But...they'd be impossible to find. I'm sure Ramsey lawyers have worked with the authorities to hide them so well, Houdini wouldn't be able to locate them."

Again, Gabriel chuckled. "Who needs Houdini? We've got someone far better, you know?"

Whatever ease Cufi had been feeling, abated with those words. He knew then with all certainty that his former *employees* would definitely be found and *dealt* with. This *someone* who was better than Houdini was why various members of the Tesano family operated with seemingly no regard or fear of discovery. Whether the Ramseys knew it or not, it had everything to do with his own miraculous escape from the Wind Rage when Fernando and Moses Ramsey were breathing down his neck. This *someone* had been labeled a myth and those who knew it to be otherwise either belonged to the organization or they were dead.

◆  ◆  ◆

Nile woke early praying her favorite heated pool would be vacant or at the very least not crowded with Hotel Brillante guests. She got her wish. The place was blissfully cleared. She was able to put in a good twenty laps which were usually as much for health of body as it was for peace of mind.

That morning, there was the added benefit of the relief of certain tensions. She'd thought of little else other than making love since Taurus Ramsey had re-entered; *no pun intended*, her world. She could scarcely look at the bed in her suite without reminders of all they'd done there. As a result, she'd opted to sleep the night before on the recliner in the apartment's alcove.

Now; looking out over the pool's calming waters, she found herself contemplating. He wanted her and foolish as it may've been, she believed his *want* was for more than sex. She felt the same things last night that she'd felt a year ago. A part of her sensed-*knew* that this was a man who'd cherish her, who'd support her through all the horrors. He'd admire and love her beauty, but he'd look beyond. He'd see the ugliness that made her and what lay beneath. He'd see the attractive packaging-the light that fought against the darkness and he'd love that too.

The tiny whispers that urged her to go to him started to gain their momentum just as she tuned into someone speaking her name.

Dena smiled more brightly when Nile's gaze snapped to her face. "Please forgive me for scaring you. I thought I'd gotten up early enough to beat anyone here." She explained as soft laughter colored her words.

Nile joined in with the laughter as well. "I had the same idea too, but you're in luck because I'm on my way out. I think I've put in enough laps to last me a week."

Dena hugged herself. "That sounds good," she sighed whipping off the robe that covered a daring bikini. The cut of the bottom offered an unhindered view of a flat belly and; against her dark skin; a crescent moon scar was vibrantly displayed.

Nile stared in a manner that was frighteningly hypnotic. Dena didn't appear to notice and left Nile with a cheery wave before sprinting toward the pool. Nile's luminous stare shined with unshed tears while a wave of nausea rumbled through her body.

# CHAPTER SIX

Darby was sure she was sleep walking when she answered the booming knock on the door of her suite.

"Hell Ny, it's barely seven a.m.," she groaned, when her friend rushed inside the room.

"We're checking out today."

"What? Why?"

"I already called the desk and informed them, so get your things packed," Nile went on alternating between wringing her hands and worrying the belt around the black terry robe.

"Hold up a minute," Darby was massaging her scalp and slowly becoming more lucid. "We haven't even spent three nights here. Besides, I'd already planned to sight see, drop in on a few of the clubs-"

"Jesus Darby! Will you just-" Nile silenced as all the breath swooshed from her lungs. She doubled over from the suddenness of it.

"Ny!" Darby called on full alert. She rushed over to catch both Nile's arms and made her sit on the sofa. "Put your head between your knees."

"Mmm mmm," Nile refused and shook her head viciously. "That makes it worse."

"Then maybe talking will help." Darby suggested none too gently. "What the devil is going on?" She hissed.

"Did you know that Taurus Ramsey bought out my show?"

"No. Not until after your dinner with him." Darby said and moved to the arm chair flanking the sofa. "I was wrapping up things with hotel personnel when he came in to look at the pieces. That's when he handed me the check for the art. Earlier I'd received a call followed by an electronic voucher signed by a Minyon Oswald-his assistant." She shrugged and fiddled with the large buttons on her candy pink pajama top. "When he walked in, he didn't appear that he wanted to be bothered. Man hands you a check for two hundred and eighty K; you do nothing to agitate him. Now will you please tell me why you're so upset?"

"He wants me. Wants *us* to…have a relationship. I think…I want to believe it's only about sex but something tells me he wants more."

"Mmm…so naturally you want to run away from him and rush back to L.A."

Nile rolled her eyes. "I don't need the sarcasm just now."

"Well shit Ny you're not making sense here. Are you on edge about it because the man's sexy and mesmerizing as heaven and you're thinkin' you couldn't possibly keep him?"

Nile snapped her fingers and winked. "Now you're talkin' *but* there's more," she added before Darby could argue. "On top of all that, I'm pretty sure that the minute he finds out who I am he may very well want to kill me."

◆    ◆    ◆

Tykira Ramsey was hunched over her easel reviewing final plans for her latest project. She was making notes to ask her crew chief Samuel Bloch during their weekly conference call, when a slew of laughter and squeals hit her ears.

Frowning, Ty left her office to hunt down the source of the elation and found that her sons and husband were at the root of it all. Tykira smiled and wasn't a bit surprised. Quaysar Ramsey drew attention wherever he went but with two beautiful three year old twins in tow, his mystique was amplified.

Of course, her mostly female staff thought so and fawned over Dinari and Dakari while covertly admiring the sinful appeal of their father.

Quay saw his wife leaning against the lobby entrance and wasted no time heading right toward her. He smoothed his hands around the waistband of her black boot cut slacks and gave her bottom a proprietary pat. He urged her back in the direction she'd come, nibbling on her neck as they returned to her office. By the time the door closed behind them, they were kissing as if starved for one another.

"Mmm Quay, Quay wait…" Ty urged, feeling his fingers on the buttons of her blouse. "We can't."

"Hush," he ordered, thumb-stroking the nipples outlined against the fabric of her lavender striped cuff shirt.

"The guys are-"

"Being spoiled by your staff who will probably try to keep them out there all day."

"Yeah…" Tykira happily agreed and gave in to her husband's persistence.

44

She was halfway stripped of the blouse when the phone began to ring. As her assistant was probably preoccupied with the twins as well, Ty knew the job as operator was now in her corner. Quay was still gnawing at her neck, his hands cupping and fondling her breasts when she laughingly answered the call.

"Good Lord," Sabra Ramsey groaned, "Will you please tell your husband to get off you for a minute so we can talk?"

"Hey girl!" Ty laughed even more when she heard the voice on the line. "Quay stop, it's Sabra."

"Uh-huh, can she call back?" He murmured, intensifying his bites upon her neck.

Ty turned in his arms. "Stop, she wants to talk."

"About?"

"Girl stuff, come on."

"Actually Ty," Sabra called, having overheard her cousin. "It's probably good he's there. Can you put me on speaker?"

"I didn't know you liked to listen Sabra." Quay teased when Ty hit the button.

"Poor Quay the older you get, the worse your jokes become. Sad thing is you don't realize it."

"Forget you. My girl likes my jokes, don't you Tyke?"

Sabra laughed. "Honey don't even bother to answer that. I know he's doing his best to um *persuade* a favorable reply."

"Damn right," Quay growled into his wife's neck.

Tykira laughed and pressed her hands against the front of Quay's red brick fleece hoody. "Y'all are too much. Come on stop and let's get serious."

"Ty's right and I don't wanna hold you guys," Sabra's voice lost some of its playfulness. "I called because I um-I'm thinking it's time to expand again and I want Ty on board for the project."

"Expansion!" Quay bellowed with laughter following. "Hell girl, you've already got too damn much on that property: casino, hotel, spa, club. What else could you want?"

"I'll think of something. I got lots more land that could stand developing." She sent a heavy sigh through the speaker then. "Besides, there're those who feel my property could use *their* personal touch and I'm not havin' it."

"Neighboring casinos?" Ty guessed.

"Hmph, I wish."

Ty fixed her husband with a concerned look.

"Alright exactly what *is* goin' on out there?" Quay asked.

Sabra waited a full five seconds before answering. "The folks sniffing around my property have Tesano connections."

Again, Quay and Ty exchanged looks. Anyone who watched the news had heard of the family whose interests involved everything from congressional seats and movie studio holdings to illegal weapons manufacture and organized crime connections.

"How do you know this?" Quay asked.

"A friend whose specialty is investigative troubleshooting, she uncovered the link."

"Have you um…spoken to anyone in the Tesano family?" Ty probed.

Sabra laughed. "I know what you're asking and the answer is no. I wouldn't call that son of a bitch if my life depended on it."

Quay and Ty exchanged looks for a third time since the conversation began. Neither bothered to mention that if Sabra had Tesanos sniffing around-her life could very well depend on it. Of course they understood her reluctance to speak with her former lover Smoak Tesano. Things between them had ended disastrously and both sides had been devastated.

"Quay? Will you talk to Quest? See if his frat brother's family is making any moves in Vegas?"

Even more drama lay in that simple request but Quay promised.

"I'll be in touch," Ty was saying once Quay had strolled off a distance from her desk. "I'll probably take a trip out there to talk and see the property myself."

Sabra almost squealed she was so delighted. "We'll make it a girl getaway and everything."

Quay stopped pacing the office and frowned toward the phone. "What the hell is that?"

"Uh uh uh Quay," Sabra scolded. "What happens in Vegas…"

Sabra let the provocative statement hang in the air and seconds later the dial tone signaled the break in the connection. The serious air still hung in Tykira's office.

"What are you thinking?" She asked.

"Could be nothing," He said though the set of his profile said otherwise.

"Are you gonna talk to Quest?"

"Yeah…though I don't think Q's talked to Pike Tesano in a while."

Ty smoothed her hands over her arms as a quick chill shimmied through her. "You think he'll even contact Pike considering all that's happened between he and…"

Quay shrugged, not needing his wife to complete the question. "Q never held Pike responsible and he'd never tell me why." He pushed both hands into the pockets of his sagging jeans to hide clenched fists. "Guess I better go see my brother." He crossed the office with intentions of kissing his wife goodbye.

After the kiss, Ty caught his sleeve. "There's something else." She swallowed her unease before it could change her mind. "These plans I'm going over," she hitched a thumb over her shoulder, "for a scientific research facility-location not specified. But the man bankrolling it all is Smoak Tesano."

♦　　♦　　♦

Nile accepted the last of the hotel receipts and turned from the desk with all intentions of making a brisk walk across the elaborate lobby and out into the courtesy limo that waited to carry her and Darby to the airport. She only got about as far as turning away from the front desk. She just managed to stop herself from bringing a hand to her mouth when she turned to find Taurus Ramsey right behind her.

"Running?" He asked, slipping a hand into his brownstone trouser pocket and watching her coolly.

Nile tried to be just as cool, but realized he probably already knew the answer to the question. "Why would you think that?" she asked anyway.

"Probably because I saw you tip the guy that put all those cases in the back of that car."

Nile bowed her head, folding her arms over the vintage yellow cardigan she wore.

"Are you afraid of me?"

She looked up again quickly. "I'm not. But a lot of us don't have scores of employees to keep a business running while we're away Mr. *Ramsey.*"

Taurus smiled, his light eyes narrowing as they raked the jeans encasing her figure. "Going back to L.A. then?"

Nile grimaced, realizing any hope of hiding out there was ruined.

Taurus didn't mention it further. Instead, he moved close to run his index finger down her cheek. Nile bit on her bottom lip when he replaced the finger with his thumb.

"Stop," she willed her legs to remain firm beneath her.

"You're not afraid of me," he repeated and remained close. "What *are* you afraid of?"

She pulled away then and fixed him with accusing eyes.

"Don't lie, not when it's written all over your face." Losing another tether on his temper, he stepped closer and clutched her arm. "I don't like this."

Nile didn't respond, but she couldn't dispute the fact that she was afraid. Strangely, what she'd discovered earlier that day wasn't at the root of her fear. Her connection to Dena Ramsey was simply the cherry on top. In Taurus Ramsey's eyes, she saw more than physical attraction. She saw tenderness and adoration. Love? She wouldn't speculate especially when that sweet emotion had no chance in hell of surviving once he discovered how her father had shattered-she suspected-a valuable portion of his own sister's life.

Nothing would matter then. It would mean nothing that while living in France, she'd spent years begging the authorities to believe her about what was going on inside her father's home in Nice. It would mean nothing that once she'd gone to the States, she tried for better luck with the authorities there and was unsuccessful. She'd been well into her twenties when she realized they'd all been bought. None of her best intentions had mattered then. They certainly wouldn't matter to this man who stood watching her with such intense emotion in his incredible eyes.

Imagining that adoring look in his eyes glossing over with a hate-filled sheen…that was what instilled true fear inside her.

Taurus released Nile's arm, massaging away any discomfort his hold might have caused. "Have a good trip." He said while brushing an airy kiss across her temple. He watched as she all but ran from the lobby and settled into the waiting limo. Then, pulling out his cell, he scrolled down the number list and made the connection.

"Taurus Ramsey for Perry Finch."

◆　◆　◆

"So you're not going to kill him?" Yvonne Wilson asked, her voice mirroring the disbelief on her face.

The gentleman relaxing behind the other side of Yvonne's desk smiled as though he were placating a small child and amused by its ignorance.

"Killing Marc Ramsey is the obvious choice," he said, "and an end that will soon visit him but unfortunately he's still got a few dues to pay."

Yvonne shook her shoulder length curls away from her face. She decided not to ask what that meant. "Is Cufi behind this?" She asked instead.

The gentleman smirked. "No."

Yvonne lost her temper then. "Dammit!" She raged and pounded a fist to her cluttered desk. "I have to know why I was asked to do this." Until then, she'd tried to accept the fact that her estranged husband was pulling all the strings and going mad because it didn't add up.

Still, she swallowed down her unease when her outburst filled the room. One didn't yell and one certainly never demanded anything of Brogue Tesano. For Yvonne however, this was all a bit too agitating. Realizing some nameless mystery man was pulling the strings to help Marc Ramsey meet a fatal end was more unnerving than believing her husband was behind it. After all, she and her people had been responsible for delivering the hated Ramsey elder, right?

48

Brogue Tesano continued to smile and appeared to be in the mood for sharing info. "Marc Ramsey is indeed suffering most horribly I can assure you of that. When we're done, he'll pray to die because his life is about to be cast into a deeper abyss than he could ever imagine." He almost purred while tugging on the cuff of the black shirt that peeked out from beneath his jacket. "This is what I do and yet I'm experiencing a certain joy in this particular job."

"Because it's Marcus Ramsey," Yvonne guessed.

Brogue's hard features tightened for the first time. "Because I have an intense aversion to people who use little girls-children at all for that matter-as objects to meet their own sick twisted needs."

Yvonne felt her hands grow slicker with a guilty sweat.

"I'm brutal when it's just a job." Brogue continued his blue stare frighteningly provocative. "I'm downright terrifying when I take pleasure in it. *But* you didn't call me here to celebrate the trials of Marc Ramsey, did you?" He leaned forward to brace his elbows on his knees. "I believe your real interests lie in a box of card keys."

Yvonne gasped, fear coursing through her then like thick slow syrup.

"Your husband has instructions to supply us with them ASAP. He knows his life is hanging by the amount of time it takes him."

"And mine?" Yvonne had to know.

Brogue nodded. "Houston and Daphne Ramseys murders were our guarantees that his life would be next." He stood. "As for you, we know you believe the keys were to *protect*- I use the term lightly- those girls. That's what Cufi told you. Truth is, his only plan for those cards was blackmail. Money, favors, it didn't matter. If Cufi Muhammad had a need, it was met...or else." He laughed softly, watching the woman absorb the information. "Think about it Yvonne. How do you think he managed to get those girls off that damn ship when the Ramseys were hot on his ass? It takes the intervention of various authoritative figures to do that, you know?" Leaning down, Brogue tapped his hand to the desk. "I've given you enough to chew on. I'll let you get back to your work and I'll get back to mine."

Yvonne waited until the man strolled from her office and then allowed her terror to take root.

◆　◆　◆

Quest finished dropping the last of the file folders into his briefcase. His left-dimpled smile made a slight appearance when he once again took note of the silence in his wife's home office. He'd worked there intentionally the night before and realized Michaela was doing her best to ignore him. She did a damn good job. Her mood hadn't improved when he'd come down to the office for his files and found her already there.

49

"How long will you give me the silent treatment?" He asked without looking her way.

No response.

Shaking his head, he eased his cell phone into his trouser pocket and turned to face her. Coolly, Mick relaxed in her desk chair with her small bare feet crossed and propped atop the desk. Massaging his neck, Quest rounded the desk and leaned down to kiss her. Mick turned her head and roused another smile from her husband.

Undeterred, he dropped kisses to her neck. He trailed several more progressively lower until his gorgeous dark face was buried in the valley between her breasts that heaved rapidly in unwilling response.

Mick pressed her lips together, but couldn't control the fluttering of her lashes when Quest tugged the zipper of her clover green hoody. Once a nipple was bared, he captured it between his lips. Mick clenched her hands into fists and passively delighted in the feel of him suckling and manipulating the ever-firming nipple.

Quest finished a while later and even took the time to pull the zipper back into place. "Forgive me," he whispered and kissed her earlobe before leaving the room.

Alone then, Mick let her head fall back on the chair and willed the fierce tingles at her core to stop…tingling. Frustrated sexually and emotionally, she threw a pen toward the door. She'd planned to extend the 'silent treatment' for another week but…well that wasn't such an easy thing to do where Quest Ramsey was concerned.

The phone rang then, sending a shriek past her lips as she jumped in her chair. Slowly, she answered.

"Yes um…Michaela Sellars-Ramsey please."

"This-this is she." Mick vaguely recognized the male voice on the other end of the line.

The man responded with a laugh. "Kayla? Ha! I couldn't believe it when my manager gave me the message."

Mick was laughing as well. "And I can't believe *you've* got managers Mr. Jazz Club Owner."

Reagan Crawford chuckled. "Guess it's in my blood," he sighed.

"And how is Mr. C?" Mick asked, referring to Reagan's father Avery Crawford who'd once owned several clubs in the Chicago area.

"So to what do I owe the honor of receiving a call from one of the Ramsey Queens?" He teased once they'd caught up for a while.

Mick laughed again. "What's this? Following the society pages now Ray? Or *these* days it could easily be the front pages." She noted her tone sobering.

"Well you're always where the action is."

"Yeah…" Mick sighed, pulling her feet off the desk to sit straight in her chair. "Anyway about why I called…there's something I need to ask."

"Anything Kayla. Just tell me what."

"Not a what-a who."

"Who."

Mick hesitated then, tapping her nails to her chin as she debated. "I need a name. The name of a man who knew someone who used to work for your father."

Ray put the pieces together easily from there. "What are you steppin' into girl?"

"My own business and something I should've stepped into a long time ago."

"Some things are best left forgotten." Ray warned. "I told you that when you asked about this before."

"And I told you-" Mick stopped herself and bristled. "Look Ray you have to *know* before you can *forget*. Now please don't argue with me Ray-not again. Not this time. With or without your help I'll find what I need. Without your help it'll be much harder."

Ray groaned after several seconds of silence. "Alright Kayla. Alright."

◆     ◆     ◆

### *Los Angeles, California~*

"I've never seen you in such a hurry to talk to Perry Finch." Nile said in the midst of a deep yawn.

Darby shrugged easily switching lanes and gears on her Mustang. "Something's up. *I've* never seen Perry not return a call that mentioned money being offered."

"What are you thinking?" Nile asked.

"Probably nothing. I don't know…maybe I'm just anxious to get the money into the slime bucket's hands and the deed to the studio into ours."

Nile rested back against the butter suede seat and hugged herself. "Maybe old Finchie is rolling between the sheets with a beautiful woman and can't be bothered with calls."

Darby smiled and exchanged a glance with Nile. Moments later, hearty laughter filled the car.

Business seemed to be chugging along as usual when Nile and Darby arrived at Finch and Associates. The assistant seemed a bit flustered when the two women approached her desk and requested her boss. After a moment however, the two were being escorted into plush office digs overlooking downtown L.A.

The sound of a flushing commode met their greeting. Shortly, Perry Finch emerged from the private bath.

Darby sneered, her green eyes coldly raking Perry's tall rotund frame. "I didn't hear you wash your hands."

Perry returned the sneer. "I didn't know you cared."

"I don't." Darby slipped both hands into the pockets of her wrap skirt. "Our business is brief so the faster we get to it the faster you can get back to jerkin' off."

"Bitch," Perry whispered.

Nile stepped up then knowing her friend's quick Irish temper combined with her fierce African American one could spell unimagined pain for the man.

"Listen Perry, we're here to settle up on our debt with you. We're here to pay you in full for the studio. So if you'd just get the deed we can get on with it."

The easy look in Perry's bloodshot brown eyes shadowed with sudden unease. Nile finally understood Darby's suspicion, but waited as if trying to silently determine what Finch was hiding.

Darby reached into her portfolio and withdrew a check. "No bullshit Perry. We're here to buy the studio."

Perry cleared his throat.

Darby slanted Nile an 'I told you so' look, then glared at Perry. "*Words* usually follow once someone clears their throat."

"I um…the studio it-it's not mine to sell. It never really was." He uttered a phony laugh and began to roll down his shirt sleeves. "Unfortunately, the true owner isn't of a mind to um, to sell it just now."

Silence resumed and Perry sighed satisfactorily as though his job was done. Without another word, he returned to his desk to happily go on with the rest of his work.

"Son of a bitch," Darby hissed charging Perry's desk while Nile charged after her.

# CHAPTER SEVEN

"I can't believe you stopped me from snappin' that pig in half!"

Darby's outburst brought a wide smile to Nile's dark face. She glanced at her best friend's busty yet slender frame. "You would've *tried*," she noted in barely concealed amusement.

Shutting off the engine, Darby leaned her head back as they remained parked in the lot outside the studio. "I'm so sorry Ny," she breathed.

Nile blinked feeling the tears suddenly pressuring her eyelids. "All's not lost yet," she tried to sound hopeful but couldn't stop her hands from sweating as she smoothed them across the front of her honey beige skirt suit. "We just need to calm down and then we go back and get him to tell us who this mystery owner is."

Darby smoothed her fingers across the ray of sunlight streaming across the steering wheel. "And then what do we do?" She asked.

Nile wouldn't be dissuaded. "It's only money, right? Everyone has a price, I'm sure…" Her voice trailed off as the attempt at optimism failed.

They left the car, regret burying them in silence. Darby headed for her office while Nile went up to the art gallery where she hoped to soothe herself among the paintings by her kids. There she let her emotions loose, crying to expel her frustration. Spent, she sat there in silence losing track of time and space until Darby called out to her.

"Guess we won't have to ask Perry who our mystery owner is after all," Darby was saying. At Nile's bewildered look, she nodded and smiled in the direction of the gallery's entryway.

Nile's bewilderment gave way to disbelief when Taurus Ramsey stepped into the room. Darby said nothing more and left them alone.

Nile rose to her feet and began smoothing her hands along the arms of her tailored blazer as if she were chilled.

"I hear you spoke to Perry," Taurus noted, slowly walking toward her.

"You? You own my-my studio?"

A grimace drew his sleek brows close. "My father did. Mine now by default after his...death." Combing fingers through his lush hair, he moved to the windows scaling the room. "I would've never known it was yours until Finch called saying he had a buyer for it but that the present tenants weren't of a mind to give it up without a fight."

Nile's temper was past the boiling point but she put on an admirable façade of calm. "That's funny because Perry told us the present owner wasn't *of a mind* to sell it."

Taurus nodded. "That's true." He said and folded his arms across the front of his long-sleeved burgundy polo shirt.

"Even after you...you knew what it was for? You still refused to sell?" Nile whispered the question and clasped her hands before her mouth. "Do you know how much hell that ass Perry Finch has put us through?"

"I can imagine."

The soft spoken acknowledgement did nothing to quell Nile's temper. "You can *imagine*? Hmph...you cold, smug, spoiled son of a bitch!" Fists clenched then, she bounded towards him and struck out against his chest blindly seeking to inflict whatever pain she could.

Taurus evaded the more serious blows easily and managed to catch Nile's wrists in one of his hands. She continued to struggle fiercely and finally cursed him in a slew of French. He jerked her once bringing an end to the flagrant obscenities.

"I'm here to change all this." He said.

"Really? You could've done that with a phone call."

"You honestly believe I'd let you go that easy?"

"Ah..." Nile began to nod in understanding. "Oh I see. So what? I have to *persuade* you, is that it? Another good romp like in Montenegro, hmm?"

Taurus moved closer towering over her while trapping her against a wall. "Well it's like you said-only sex. No...no what was it? Meaningless gratification."

"Bastard," Nile hissed but in reality she was angrier with herself for having her own careless and dishonest words used against her. She took stock then of how close they were and how very much she wanted to melt against him. How very much she wanted to enjoy his touch again-meaningless or otherwise.

"What do you want me to do?"

"Come with me."

"No."

"No is it? You sure?" He challenged, his heavenly features growing more sinful then. "And here you've got me thinkin' you'd do anything to save those kids."

Nile winced feeling her wrists jerk reflexively against his hold. It was true-the truest thing about her. And in that truth, she was about to *do* one more thing that would make her like her slime of a father.

"I have to tell Darby." She explained frowning up when he refused to release her.

"No need." He said.

"My-my purse."

"Already in my truck thanks to Darby," he informed her and gave her a tug when she looked panicky. He waited for her to calm, and then went to the doorway of the gallery.

Nile followed his lead, but stopped just short of meeting him. She gave the gallery one last look, and then preceded him through the door.

♦   ♦   ♦

"I didn't pack anything," Nile breathed. Her eyes were wide as small moons while taking in the magnificent white jet with the distinctive silver R- painted and circled on the fin.

Taurus' grin was slow and not at all reassuring. "Don't worry about it." He said.

Nile managed a wavering smile. "You're right. I guess I won't need clothes much."

Taurus grunted a short laugh which was difficult considering his every thought at that point was focused on her without her clothes.

The laugh only told Nile that she was right. Instead of dwelling on all the sexual favors she'd agreed to perform for the foreseeable future, she focused on her kids. Assurance lay in the knowledge that after this trip, the studio would be theirs.

Taurus parked the rugged Land Rover a distance from the jet. When he left the truck and came around to escort her out, Nile stubbornly refused to take the hand he offered. He kept his hand extended, proving he could be just as stubborn as she. Once she'd slapped her palm against his and scooted off the seat, he wouldn't let her pass.

"You can change your mind." He said.

She wouldn't meet his gaze. "No I can't."

Taurus leaned against the side of the Rover and watched her walk off toward the jet. Bowing his head, he thanked God for letting her buy his bluff. His only goal was to have her see that there was more between them than meaningless gratification. Using the studio to get her to come with him was low, but she wouldn't have agreed otherwise. She would have never walked out the door with him had she known he'd already signed over the deed and it; along with the money they'd been prepared to pay, were safely tucked away in Darby Ellis' office.

Then again, maybe she would've left with him, he thought. His hands settled into the pockets of his sagging jeans as he followed her to the aircraft. She might've come if she'd known, but it would've only been out of gratitude and he wanted far more than that.

Smiling broadly then, Taurus nodded toward the man who approached him. "Bern," he greeted the captain of the jet.

"I'm assuming this won't be a round trip." Bernard Hoke teased.

"And why would you assume that?" Taurus propped a fist beneath his chin and pretended to be confused.

Bernard's dark eyes narrowed when he looked back toward the plane. "Man could lose himself for an eternity with a beauty like that to enjoy." He almost murmured in awe while watching Nile across the tarmac.

Taurus' gaze was set in the same direction. "What's an eternity when you've already lost your heart?"

Bernard laughed then. "I'll pray for you man!" He clapped Taurus' back before they prepared to board.

♦      ♦      ♦

### *Near Invernesshire, Scotland~*

Nile's face had been frozen in a state of disbelief since they'd left the jet. Her unease had flown right off the charts once she'd discovered where they were headed. They'd been driven from the jetport through Edinburg and onward into the country with its vast fields of heather and moss. Those fields seemed to stretch on forever, past lakes and brooks that encircled glorious manor houses and cottages. When they drove past a castle perched atop a massive cliff, Nile could no longer contain her silence.

"How long do you plan to keep me here?" She breathed, her eyes still glued to the scenery.

"As long as it takes," he promised and then left the car when it drew to a halt.

"No need for that Mr. C," Taurus urged the driver.

Colin Bradenton was about to leave the car in order to escort his passengers. "Should I send up the missus?" He asked while settling back behind the wheel.

"No need for that either," Taurus patted Colin's shoulder. "We should be fine for the first two days at least. I'll try not to burn down the place before then," he promised with a sly grin.

Colin chuckled before glancing in the rearview mirror. "Is she the one lad?"

Taurus nodded without hesitation. "She doesn't believe it though."

"Ah and you brought her here to…persuade her, eh?"

Taurus tried to join in with Colin's devilish chuckling but couldn't manage it. "I brought her here to fall in love with me." He admitted and then shook his head toward the older man. "I'm a fool, right?"

"Aye…that you are lad, but you're a fool in love and there's no better kind." He said, his voice lilting with a promising tenderness. Tugging on the brim of his worn wool cap, he glimpsed into the rearview once more. "You'll be fine," he added and squeezed Taurus' hand once more.

Nile had already left the car and was standing along the wide cobblestone drive. Eyes narrowed in awe, they wandered across the stone manor. The vast fields they'd passed on the way in surrounded the place in a sea of grass and clusters of trees. Jagged cliffs lent to the beauty of the overcast environment. She jumped at the feel of Taurus' lean muscular form behind her. Keeping her composure, she allowed him to lead her toward the house.

Inside, she was again floored by the loveliness that greeted her. Elegant tapestries and provocative portraits covered the stone walls while exquisite rugs were visible upon the gleaming wood floors of the entryway and other front rooms.

Taurus leaned against a carved front post of the banister and watched Nile looking around. God he could watch her for the rest of his life, he believed and prayed he would have the chance. Nile noticed him staring and mistook his look for anything other than love or adoration.

Forcing her bubble of shame back into its usual hiding place far below the surface, she unbuttoned the short waist blazer and shimmied out of the matching skirt while kicking off her pumps.

Taurus was struck silent and could only look on in helpless fascination. His brilliant light stare raked her half clad body countless times as if he were trying to view as much as possible before the moment passed. Nile closed the distance separating them and didn't stop until she had him pinned against the newel post. Standing on her toes, she brought her mouth to his and kissed him with an eager passion.

Taurus winced as desire fanned through him and he willed his legs to remain strong beneath him. Tortured moans crowded his throat then, his hands filled with her flawless licorice dark body. Turning the situation to suit him, he trapped Nile against the banister and deepened the kiss. His tongue stroked and scraped the ridge of her teeth while one hand disappeared beneath the open blazer to press against the small of her back. For a time, he ignored the voice that chanted 'not this way'. He only wanted a few more seconds to inhale her scent and drink in the sweet essence of her kiss-only a few more seconds to pretend she was his. Truly his.

"Nile…" he murmured next to her throat. Arrogant confidence built inside him when her shaky moans reached his ears.

Just like that she was drowning amidst the waves of her need for him. Greedily, her hands swirled throughout his gorgeous hair. Wanton cravings sent her arching and grinding herself against the subtle power of his body. She was seconds away from begging him to do what she ached for, but it was then that she tuned into him calling her name and asking her to stop.

Confusion clouded her eyes as she searched his face. "Isn't this what you want?"

*God yes*, he confirmed silently and squeezed his eyes shut against the erotic heaving of her breasts practically spilling from the lacy mocha bra. He was insane to urge her back, he acknowledged that. However, he was after something more alluring and longer lasting than sex. With a strength every man in his family would have admired, he set away the half dressed beauty.

"Your room is uh-the um second on the left. Top of the stairs," he finished and extracted himself from their embrace. "Dinner's in three hours." He called absently across his shoulder.

Alone on the staircase, Nile struggled to catch her breath and her sanity. In her own absent manner, she collected her clothes and searched out the room he'd instructed. Once there, she didn't bother to dress as the room was toasty warm from the blaze in the beautifully designed hearth. She curled up on the settee before the fire and thought about what had just happened and what to make of it. Turning on her side, she closed her eyes and decided not to make much of it. After all, they'd just had a long flight-perhaps he meant to wait until after dinner. By then he would have eaten and rebuilt his stamina. Something inside her tingled naughtily at the thought. Anymore stamina and walking would be impossible she mused, recalling the power in his touch. She snuggled down onto the settee and tried to dismiss the memory. A nap was in order and it was no surprise that her dreams starred Taurus Ramsey.

◆    ◆    ◆

The fire blazed more brightly in the room though it had burned down considerably. Nile realized she'd dozed almost two hours. She pushed off the settee and stretched feeling unexpectedly rejuvenated. She crossed the room to gaze out over the landscape which was a bit darker than before she'd napped. Checking her watch, she saw that there was little more than an hour before dinner and decided on a shower.

Sighing, Nile gathered her suit. Hanging it would be best if they were to serve her for the duration of the strange trip. She was headed for the closet in search of a hanger. The clothes drifted from her weakened hands when she whipped open the door. Lovely garments for every occasion filled the closet- all with tags still attached and displaying her size.

"Mon Dieu, what's he up to?" She breathed, smoothing the chiffon sleeves of an evening gown across her cheek.

With renewed interest fueling her, she inspected the bureau and found that it was filled with new under things and lounge wear. A knock upon the door sent her whirling around in surprise. Stumbling on weak legs, she grabbed up the blazer and held it before her chest.

Taurus lost track of what he'd come to say when Nile opened the door. He drank in the sight of her before tracking down what remained of his voice.

"Do you have everything you need?" He asked his tone thoroughly adorable in its hushed tone.

Nile dragged her eyes away from his face and glimpsed the closet. "I'm not sure…the clothes…"

"Are yours." He explained, tilting his head as his unnerving light stare judged her reaction. "There're suitcases under the bed. You can take everything with you when you leave."

"Why?"

He shrugged, propping a shoulder against the doorjamb. He felt an uncharacteristic bout of embarrassment at telling her he'd bought her a new wardrobe because he been fantasizing about seeing her wear every piece that now dwelled inside room. "When I asked you to come with me, I didn't give you time to pack."

"You didn't ask." Nile whispered.

He bowed his head. "Would you have come if I did?"

"Guess you'll never know."

"My loss."

Silence was irrelevant then, for their gazes spoke volumes.

At last, Taurus trailed the back of his hand around her jaw, down the length of her neck and across her collarbone. He focused on where his thumb brushed the pulse at her throat and then lower to the curve of her breast exposed above the edge of the blazer she clutched.

"I'll let you get dressed," he said pushing off the jamb and leaving her with a soft smile.

Nile leaned against the spot he'd just vacated. She lost track of how much time had passed. When she snapped to and raced into the hall to ask him to stay, he was gone.

# CHAPTER EIGHT

"You cook?" Nile remarked, obviously quite surprised.

"I heat." Taurus corrected. "The couple who looks after the place-remember the man driving the car before?" He watched Nile give a quick nod. "Colin Bradenton. His wife Moira keeps me fed whenever I come here." He strolled toward the stove, his brown leather flip flops softly clapping at the polished floor. "I always let Miss Moira know when I'm coming in and she prepares dinner for a few nights out."

Nile fiddled with the split sleeve of her violet and rose embroidered caftan dress. Her expression was thoughtful as she followed him across the spacious kitchen. "It's interesting how you speak of them-not as chauffer or caretaker, housekeeper or maid. You act as if they're a couple simply doing you a favor." She noted, not bothering to hide how very much that impressed her.

Taurus shrugged. "I've known 'em for years." He spoke with a somber tone filtering his words. "Sometimes they were more like parents than my own." He shared and then nodded toward the dining area. "Let's eat."

The hearty beef vegetable stew and thick biscuits were *heated* to perfection. An easy silence filled the cozy alcove in the kitchen where they'd chosen to dine. The lights had been dimmed and candlelight used instead. The outline of rolling hills and brush was just visible against the dark.

"I wanted to tell you how sorry I am about your parent's death. Your sister told me in Montenegro." Nile added when Taurus looked up at her suddenly.

"Thank you." He spoke softly but looked down again quickly lest she notice the muscle jumping in his jaw as he reigned in a sudden surge of anger over the thought of his parents.

"Well this is an incredible house." Nile changed subjects in a sarcastically refreshing tone and joined Taurus when he laughed.

"I know you think it's over the top," he said following her gaze across the high ceilings and the rafters supporting it. "But…as most places here *are* over the top, I don't feel so bad about it."

"I suppose you can get away with it." She chuckled and eased a lock of hair behind her ear. "Not too sure I could say the same if you'd seen fit to buy that old abandoned castle I saw on the way in."

Taurus' laughter that time was honest and infectious warming the inviting kitchen with its depth. "It won't be abandoned for long if one of my neighbors has his say."

Nile slathered butter to a corner of her third biscuit. "Sounds like an interesting story," she noted.

Taurus helped himself to a swig of Killian's Red and nodded. "Kraven DeBurgh. He's leasing now, but intends to buy the place. *But* he's being stalled by the town because he wants to turn it into a hunting manor. The drama over it all is interesting considering much of the town is related." He shrugged, running a hand across the lightweight gray sweatshirt he sported. "All that in-fighting makes me feel like I'm home."

Nile knew the words weren't spoken in fun, but felt it best they not dwell there. "Kraven DeBurgh…sounds like quite a man." She mused.

Taurus grinned, his easy mood returning. "You'll have the chance to see for yourself. The town holds a huge gala to bring in the fall of the year. Kraven's agreed to host it at the castle-takes place in about three weeks."

Nile's spoon fell into her stew.

Taurus pretended not to notice her reaction and resumed his eating with hearty delight.

Later, Nile and Taurus ventured into the den that encompassed the entire west end of the first floor. The area had a rustic, masculine appeal yet remained warm and inviting. Nile could scarcely pull her eyes away from the bay window that; by day, offered a view of the never ending back fields.

"Why'd you buy this place?" She asked when Taurus walked in carrying a tray of coffee and cake.

"I met Kraven through business and we struck up a friendship," he began to explain while setting the tray to the heavy pine coffee table before the fireplace. "I visited him here one year and fell in love with the place and the people-they've sort of adopted me." He offered a wistful smile and shrugged. "It felt like nothing I'd ever known, not even from my own parents."

"Not even from your mother?" Nile couldn't help but ask.

"She tried," he admitted joining Nile on the sofa as he poured the coffee. "All she went through with my father made it hard though. When my sister and I were kids she went along with his views never questioning the way he tried to raise us to be perfect. I think she was striving for some form of perfection in her own life and couldn't admit she'd fallen way short."

"I don't think my father was interested in raising me to be perfect," Nile confessed and shook her head. "I don't know why he wanted to raise me at all actually. The one good thing he'd done for me in my youth was finding a wife who gave a damn."

Taurus sat back against the heavily cushioned forest green sofa. He was intrigued and listened intently as Nile went on.

"...she wasn't my real mother, but she was so loving...I felt like we'd always been together which was important since I'd lost my own mother so young." A wry smile curved her lips then. "Wasn't until I grew older and realized how much of a lie my real life was..." she trailed away intentionally and leaned forward to let her parted hair shield one side of her face. "You're very lucky you had a sister to share things with."

"You're right," Taurus said though his voice held the same pensive tone as the look in his deep set eyes. "But I always felt like she went through a lot more than she ever told me." He raked a hand through his unruly hair and smiled. "I guess being older...she wanted to spare me. I don't know..."

Nile however, *did* know and the reality made her tremble.

Taurus noticed. "Hey?" He leaned over to tug at the ruffled hem of her dress. "Sorry about that. I guess my family story isn't the only one filled with drama best left forgotten."

Nile could only shake her head, words were impossible. She smoothed her hands across her arms to ward off the chill that kissed them through the violet embroidered sleeves.

"Here," Taurus grunted and left the sofa to stoke the fire. Once the flames were snapping fiercely, he pushed a steamy mug of coffee into her hands.

Nile's lashes fluttered as the aroma of the delicious berry blend teased her nostrils. She smiled when he kissed her forehead and sat close.

"I do apologize," he spoke after a bit of silence, "my last name and all the crap connected with it was a reason why I didn't tell you who I was. People hear the name Ramsey and they think of all the scandals-none of the good. We've done plenty." He said in a voice as firm as the look he cast toward the glowing flames in the hearth.

"I know," Nile agreed while nodding. "It's hard for anyone seriously interested in child welfare not to know about all your family's done to help." She sipped the coffee and massaged her palms around the heated ceramic mug. "I wondered or hoped you all would do more in California. The teen center in Malibu does such incredible things for those kids-your family should be proud. The center was one of the reasons why I kept going with my studio-there're so many monsters out there waiting to pounce on a child unless there's someone to stop them."

"That the only reason you do it?" Taurus fiddled with the drawstring of his lounge pants. He smiled at the confusion in her eyes. "Most people have events in their pasts that fuel passion like that." He explained.

Nile looked down into her mug. "Is that why your cousins do it?" She asked, hoping to shift attention from herself.

"The twins?" Taurus spoke with honest laughter in his voice. "Those two couldn't have had more stable parents but I think they saw close up what *unstable* ones could do to kids. I guess that fuels most of it for them."

"Hmph, unstable parents, I've certainly seen my share of those." Nile thought of her kids before thinking of herself. "Hell, I *had* those unstable parents myself." *Still do*, she added silently.

Taurus took advantage of the moment to toy with a glossy lock of her hair. "You want to talk about it?"

"Ha! Not unless I'm being forced to."

"Understood."

The crackle of the fire filled the otherwise silent room for a time. Eventually they were both reclining on the sofa with their feet propped upon the coffee table.

"What was the other reason?"

It was Taurus' turn to look confused. "Other reason?"

Nile looked over at him. "You said your last name was *a* reason why you didn't tell me who you were but it wasn't *the* reason. Was there another?"

Taurus took her hand and turned it over in his. "Because you asked me not to and you seemed terrified when you asked and I didn't want you to be terrified. I realized I'd do anything to keep that look out of your eyes."

Nile felt her heart pounding in the middle of her throat. "Is it so easy for women to get what they want from you?"

He grinned bashfully in response, but sobered before he looked at her. "No, but it's easy for you."

She'd forgotten how very soothing and persuasive his voice was when the softness overwhelmed the rough. She could've melted as much from the hypnotic heat of it as from the heat of the flames popping around the grand hearth.

Taurus heard his voices of reason telling him to back off and he promised to do so. First, he wanted a second to kiss her-only a second.

Nile's gasp mingled with a needy cry when she felt the crush of his lips upon her own. Eagerly, her tongue sought his and became a willing captive inside his mouth. A helpless sound swelled in his chest as he rose to smother her back into the sofa.

*Perhaps a bit longer than a second,* Taurus decided and deepened the kiss.

Nile was weakened body and soul but felt no shame in letting him control the scene. Taurus understood that his voices of reason were in serious danger of being ignored. He prayed she would whisper just a word of resistance. She didn't and soon all he could hear was the roar inside his head that urged conquest. Moments later, his face was buried in the crook of her neck and he was filling his hands with her breasts.

He heard her voice just as he moved to unravel the bodice strings of the dress that had teased him all evening. There were no whispers to stop or wait only that he put his mouth on her. He groaned when she begged the request close to his ear. Clenching trembling fists, he willed himself to back off...not yet...not yet...

"It's late," his voice was thoroughly rough again as he worked to catch his breath. "We should go on up."

Nile blinked, forbidding herself from telling him that it was only past eight and demanding that he tell her what was going on. Still, curiosity gleamed on her face as her expressive dark gaze tried to read his expression only to find that impossible.

She followed his lead up the massive stone steps that curved from the rear of the den. Silence reigned until they reached her bedroom door.

"Good night," he said and turned away without another word.

"Taurus what are you doing?" She blurted, forced to give into the confusion and frustration that warred inside her. The dimples graced either side of her mouth when she practically laughed at the look he sent her. He appeared as though he had no idea what she meant.

"Have you forgotten why I'm here? That you told me I had to come with you if I wanted my studio?"

Taurus shrugged, slipping both hands into his cotton lounging pants as he leaned against the wall.

"Well?" She challenged.

"I remember."

"And?"

"And what, Nile?"

She did laugh then and her temper was fueled by the dire need to backhand his beautiful face. "What? Is this-this waiting all part of the humiliation process?"

Taurus studied his feet one crossed over the other in the flip flops. At last, he decided to stop torturing her.

64

"I didn't bring you here to humiliate you which is precisely why the deed to your studio is safe with Darby."

Nile's mouth was a perfect O.

"Along with the check you were going to give to Perry Finch."

Nile braced her hand against the wall for support.

"You did all I asked by coming with me." He shook his head just slightly. "Whether you'd come with me or not, the studio would've still been yours." Grimacing then, he returned his focus to his feet. "You were never in any danger of losing it and I should apologize for ever threatening you with it."

"Why?" Nile breathed, watching his entrancing smile flash once more.

"If it isn't obvious by now, maybe; by the time we leave this place, it will be. Good night Nile."

"Wait," she called, catching his hand as he pushed off the wall. "Thank you," she said.

Nodding quickly, Taurus had every intention of obeying the orders to go that were screaming inside his head. Instead, he stood there further captivated by her wide eyes and every other element that comprised her extraordinary face. He accepted then that the night would end with them in bed together-in bed with her knowing it wasn't a place she had to be in order to keep what meant everything to her.

His hand slipped out of hers and he grasped her wrist with a deft quickness. Nile was afraid to speak or move lest he change his mind again. Reacting; unfortunately, was not a thing she could resist doing not when his kisses bore such a scandalous resemblance to making love. He released her hand to curl his fingers inside the bodice of her dress. Meanwhile, his tongue stroked slowly, lazily, exploring every inch of her mouth.

"Please don't stop this time," she shamelessly urged, delighting in the sensational feel of her breasts heaving against his fingers.

Taurus had no intentions of doing anything so insane. Inside of five seconds, Nile's dress was laying in a wrinkled heap upon the floor. He hoisted her against his chest and crossed the threshold into her room.

Nile buried her hands in his incredible hair. Trembling with a mixture of desire and anticipation, she kicked off her slippers and grazed her toes along the long length of his leg. She felt him undo the clasp of her bra and moments later she wore nothing but a pair of lacy black bikinis.

Taurus grumbled a curse when he had her on the bed. Suddenly, the lightweight cotton shirt he wore felt a bit too confining. Quickly, he rose above her and practically ripped it off his back.

Nile bit on her bottom lip staring in wonder as her nails raked the carved array of abs and pects that flexed impressively beneath her touch. He was covering her again with his powerful frame. Ravenously, he feasted on her breasts, beneath her breasts…suckling the ever firming nipples until they stood firm and seemed to yearn for more. He worked his mouth down her body, stopping briefly to tongue her bellybutton and the crescent shaped scar that marred the otherwise flawless dark of her skin. Her need for him was so intense, she felt orgasmic even then and moaned her disapproval when a wave of moisture soaked her panties. Taurus' perfect teeth nipped at the waistband of the lingerie and tugged it away in expert fashion.

"Jesus," he muttered.

"I'm sorry," Nile whispered squeezing her eyes shut when he spotted her need.

"Don't you dare," he refused to accept the apology and winked when she smiled.

Nile pressed her head back into the already tangled bed covers as the orgasmic pleasure re-emerged inside her. His tongue was plundering the moist, fragrant depths of her sex. His skill had her gasping and laughing her delight. She trembled so fiercely he had to hold her almost painfully tight to pleasure her. Nile welcomed it, draping one leg across his shoulder as she rotated herself on his tongue.

She was in the midst of her second orgasm when she felt the length and width of an organ vastly stiffer than his tongue. Helplessly aroused, she threw her arms above her head and played in her hair while twisting and arching to meet every drive of his hips.

Taurus cupped a breast and nibbled upon the firm satiny expanse while he plundered the heat of her body. When she trembled overmuch, he set his knee in place across her thigh. The gesture both stilled her and increased the wondrous penetration. Taurus lost his ability to keep his restraint in check.

The feel of him coming inside her stimulated a third orgasm then. Their cries of satisfaction and desire mingled throughout the room and upper level of the house. Then, within minutes of each other, they drifted off into a deep, contented slumber.

♦　　♦　　♦

Nile woke just after dawn. She wasn't surprised to find herself alone in bed and headed downstairs for coffee. The timer had been set for six a.m. so when she arrived in the massive kitchen around 6:30am a nice hot cup was hers for the taking. She enjoyed the creamy brew while taking in the lush hills capped with waves of heavy fog. Observing the dim haunting beauty of the environment, Nile revisited the events from the previous evening. Soon however, those thoughts threatened to make her as hot as the coffee she drank.

Movement registered then and she turned to find the object of her thoughts strolling barefoot into the kitchen. He wore only a pair of wrinkled sleep pants and looked deliciously tousled in his sleepy state. Nile felt her palms react to the memory of his gorgeous hair filling them. To occupy herself, she prepared another cup of coffee and had it ready to push into his hands when he met her at the counter. In silence, they enjoyed the view and the coffee.

Then Taurus set his cup aside, relieved Nile of hers and; an instant later, Nile found herself joining the mugs on the counter. Her cries filled the kitchen as Taurus filled his hands with her body. He didn't bother to remove the scant nightie she'd thrown on to come downstairs. He massaged her breasts through the material and suckled her nipples until they were outlined against it.

Nile trembled when his persuasive hands traveled the length of her thighs urging the gown up as they went. Taurus was indeed newly starved for her and took her eagerly and with complete control. Nile was as aroused by the feel of him inside her as she was by the strength he used to hold her. Once he'd finished with her atop the counter, he carried her with him to one of the heavy wooden chairs at the dining table and replayed the act. The table rounded out the interlude and Nile was unable to even raise herself up from its polished surface as she was so thoroughly spent.

No worries were necessary, for Taurus carried her upstairs and put her back to bed shortly after.

"Séjour." *Stay* she'd uttered reaching out for him when he would've left her to rest. Her heart pounded with a fierceness that almost frightened her when he joined her in bed. She realized then how *newly starved* she was for his closeness.

# CHAPTER NINE

Taurus sat on the edge of Nile's bed quite content on waiting for her to awaken. As if in awe, he studied her features relaxed in sleep. He knew he'd give anything to know if he had the smallest hope of having her feelings run even slightly parallel to his own. On cue, it seemed, her lashes fluttered and her eyes focused right on his.

"Are you okay?" He asked softly.

She nodded. "I am."

"Hungry?"

"I…" Her eyes shifted towards the food laden cart at the foot of the bed. Then she looked up at him.

"I owe you."

Nile laughed at his explanation. "I think you've more than made up for it."

"Nothing makes up like food," he argued and sent her a playful wink when her expression clearly stated her disagreement. He left the bed and went to fix her a plate of croissants, fruit, cheeses and seasoned hash browns.

"What do you expect will come from all this?" Nile asked as she watched him pour juice.

He shrugged. "You mean besides all this gratification?"

Nile couldn't help but smile. "But you know that really is all that can come of it."

Taurus clenched his jaw, but kept his temper in check. "You honestly believe that, I guess?"

"Don't you?"

He set down the pitcher of orange juice and came to lean over her in bed fisting both hands on either side of her. "You know my last name and yet here you are…I'd say anything's possible."

She steeled herself against shivering. "I know your secrets but you don't know mine."

"So? Tell me. Why?" He asked when she only shook her head. Sitting then, he took her chin in his hand and made her look at him. "Remember when I asked before if you were afraid of me? Were you lying?" He probed, watching her closely and knowing it would kill him to know that she was.

"No," she sighed, curving her hand about the one that cupped her chin. "I'm not afraid but...well I...I can't."

Taurus wouldn't press it farther just then and gave her chin a squeeze before he stood. "Eat up and then get dressed. I have something to show you."

◆　　◆　　◆

"Mon Dieu," Nile breathed in complete disbelief as she stood in a small storage shed just off from the stables. The shed was filled with an assortment of paints, fillers, canvases, brushes and anything else a starving or well-fed artist could need or want.

"Just look around," Taurus urged. Effortlessly, he placed a massive stone before the shed's door to keep it open. "Let me know if you need anything else and we can have it here within a day or two."

"Why?" She whispered her hands meeting her jean clad thighs with a soft clap. "Why all this? I'd have been happy with an easel and a few brushes."

Taurus leaned against the heavy wooden door. "I want you to have everything you need."

"The money you must've spent," Nile breathed, her dark eyes narrowed as she studied the supplies more closely. "And I have so much of this..." she threw him a sly look. "If I'd been *allowed* to pack I could've saved you a few dollars."

Taurus smiled at the tease and followed her deeper into the shed. When Nile turned and found herself secured between the wall and his body, she felt a chill of anticipation kiss her skin beneath the fuzzy cinnamon brown cardigan she wore.

"I would've done this anyway," he assured her, taking her hand and pressing it to the front of his Tuskegee sweatshirt. "I want to take care of you, at least while we're here. Humor me, will you?"

"Well...in that case *thank you*, thank you so very much." She went on, laying the syrupy sweetness on thick. Smiling saucily, she continued. "I honestly don't know what I would've done if you hadn't come to my rescue."

"That's more like it," he growled approvingly and happily accepted the kiss she offered.

The humor dwindled then as the light kiss easily shimmied into something more provocative. Nile lost her hands in his hair and deepened the kiss when she felt his fingers skirting her skin beneath the cardigan. Her need for him rose that time at a scary pace. Taurus resisted when she took his hand and curled his fingers into the waistband of her jeans. Grinning devilishly at the pure innocence radiating from her lovely gaze, he pulled her from the wall.

"Paint," he ordered. "I'll see you for lunch!" He called over his shoulder and left the shed like the devil was at his back.

♦　　♦　　♦

## Seattle, Washington

Johari Frazier woke with a yawn and frowned while staring at the blaring red numbers on the clock that read 4:42a.m. Her head fell back to the pillow and she smoothed a hand across the massive bed in search of Moses. Realizing she was alone, her head snapped up and the frown returned. She took a slow scan of the bedroom and could see him standing nude and unmindful of the cold as he leaned against the doors leading to the balcony. She watched him for a while, not caring for the pensive element darkening his striking profile as he looked out over the view. He must've felt her watching for he turned then and looked directly at her.

"What's wrong?" She called, turning to her stomach and bracing her elbows on the pillows.

Moses left the doorway and crossed to the bed. Taking a seat on the edge, he clasped his fingers between hers once she'd turned over to face him.

"Did I wake you?" He asked.

Johari shrugged. "I'm used to having you smother me, so I know when you're gone."

"Sorry," he said, absently fiddling with a few sandy red tendrils that had escaped the loose ball atop her head.

Jo grimaced. "I'd like an explanation instead. You've been acting weird since the will reading-after that call you got."

"Just business."

She nodded. "Right and I'm your lover not your business partner."

He squeezed her hand and pressed it to his mouth. "You're my lover and partner in every way. But this is something I need to keep to myself for a while. Can you understand that?"

"I can, but I'd just feel better if you had someone to talk to."

"Fern knows."

Jo sat up a bit more. "So it *does* have something to do with that trip you took?"

Moses massaged his eyes. "Twig," he groaned.

"Alright, alright I won't press."

He grinned, his gorgeous dark features softening with the love he felt for her. "I like it when you press," he said letting his fingers trail beneath the sheet sliding off her breasts. "Just don't press about *this*."

Johari nodded and cleared her throat in a playful manner. "I'll just revert back to lover mode, then."

Moses' eyes followed the tail of his fingers about Johari's breast when he spoke. "What would you say about changing that mode?"

Confused, Jo simply stared and waited for clarification.

*Clarification* came in the form of Moses leaning close and pressing his mouth to hers. "Be my wife?" he asked.

Johari gasped giving him the chance to kiss her deeply. The kiss practically robbed her breath. "Are you-are you sure?" She managed while thrusting her tongue against his.

"I've always been sure," he told her then, pulling back to study her face. "Unless I'm too late and you've changed your mind."

"That could never happen. I love you." She whispered.

"I love you." Moses reciprocated in spite of the fact that his heart was in his throat.

They sealed the plan with another kiss.

◆　　◆　　◆

Nile was putting the finishing touches to a landscape piece. Her face was a study in concentration as she bit her bottom lip and focused on the cluster of brush she worked on.

She'd received every artist's dream gift a few days earlier from Taurus. From there, she set out to challenge herself by painting outside her realm of expertise. The highland beauty she gazed upon each day became her inspiration and she found herself trying to capture as much of it on canvas as possible. Part of her wondered if having Taurus in such close proximity had allowed her to focus her talents on other subjects.

An unexpected surge of heat had her tugging at the mauve turtleneck she wore. It was a wonder she could focus on anything non-erotic with all the new *heated* images he'd put inside her head. The last few days had been like a dream. They talked, made love well into the night and morning. Taurus lived up to his word when he said he wanted to care for her. She had never felt more pampered.

Nile felt him near then, watching her. She didn't even have to turn her head. When she did, she found him holding a basket in one hand-a gray and black fleece blanket in the other. She watched as the wind whipped his hair lifting it fiercely about his face. His gaze sparkled with a brilliance she'd come to treasure. Nile realized she loved him-loved him body and soul. Before her thoughts went any deeper, she heard him asking if she could take a break.

"Just finishing up!" she called back with a nod.

Taurus' stare narrowed as he moved closer to observe her work.

"What do you think?" Nile asked in an almost timid voice.

Tilting his head this way and that, Taurus set a quizzical expression in place. "Which way is up?"

Unable to stop her laughter, Nile leaned forward and rapped his calf with her fist.

"I know just the wall in my office where I want to put it." He said.

"Don't lie," Nile urged her expression serious.

"True talent comes through in anything you put your heart into."

"I wonder…" Nile breathed, turning his words over in her head. "I don't know how much of my heart is in what I do."

"I don't believe that," Taurus said as he went about setting out lunch. "I can't believe you even feel that way especially with the way people rave over your work. They love what you do."

"Sex sells," she replied while crawling over to claim her spot on the large blanket. She glimpsed the frown he sent her way and smirked. "My…*work* doesn't fuel passion in my heart. It clears my head of things I wish I'd never seen."

"Tell me," he breathed drawing up jean clad legs to rest his elbows across his knees.

Nile focused on the overcast skies and the beauty rolled out before her. "When I was a child I saw…purely *adult* things," she sent him a meaningful look, "on an almost daily basis." She rolled her eyes away from the view. "There was an excitement in seeing those things that made me…giddy." She grimaced at the admission. "Somewhere deep inside I knew it was wrong-wrong to see."

"And seeing was all you ever did?" Taurus asked, rage building inside him as the words left his mouth.

"I was never touched that way as a child," she assured him her tone as stoic as the look in her dark eyes. *I saw others my age…* she couldn't admit that aloud.

"But you felt guilty for what those…images made you feel?" He guessed.

"Painting helps me purge it in a way I guess-in a *healthy* way."

"Well I guess making crazy amounts of money from it is about as healthy as you can get." Taurus teased and smothered her hand in his.

"It shames me to sell it. Darby thinks I'm crazy." She shared.

"I can understand why you'd feel that way."

Nile blinked. "You can?" She marveled sitting up a bit straighter as she watched him.

Taurus gave her hand a reassuring squeeze. "You hate what you saw because of the way it made you feel," he speculated warming the back of her hand as he rubbed it across the black knit sweater he wore. "What you saw as a child has given you the ability to create things people will pay obscene amounts of cash to own and that cash allowed you to give kids-who also see things they shouldn't-something few would even be privy to."

"And here I thought I'd exchange my erotica brush for a landscape one," she teased trying to hide how touched and more in love with him his words made her.

"Is there room for both?" He asked.

Nile wrinkled her nose while waving her hands about her. "I fear I may run out of ways to paint trees and hills."

Taurus' grip around her hand tightened once more while he drew her close. "Guess I'll just have to give you a few more examples then."

Nile was on her back a moment later and being given an exquisite view of yet another landscape subject: the sky. A sweet delicious interlude followed and was completed by a delicious lunch on the windblown hillside.

◆　◆　◆

"It'll be just a minute love."

Nile rolled her eyes even as a smile curved her mouth. "I completely disagree because the moment I *smelled* it, I wanted to sit and eat the entire pot."

"Oh…" Moira Bradenton softly scolded while waving Nile forward and dipping her ladle into a steaming pot.

Whatever the creation, it had Nile craving all of it as she'd expected it would. Moira blew across the surface of the creamy soup and then presented the spoon to Nile.

Bits of onion, mushroom and celery mingled with tiny broccoli and potato chunks and morsels of spinach. The wonderfully seasoned cream concoction slid down Nile's throat and warmed her tummy with a cozy rush of satisfaction.

"Bowl," Nile ordered frowning when Moira laughed and ushered her out. "How long?" she inquired refusing to budge past the table.

Moira wiped her hands on the crisp navy apron that covered most of the beige dress she wore beneath it. "Dinner tonight," she announced.

"Tonight? But it's practically done."

"That's right-*practically* done. Dinner tonight."

Nile grimaced but decided against arguing further. Moira Bradenton had tortured both she and Taurus relentlessly for the past several days with her fabulous dishes. In spite of the torture however, Moira and Nile had become surprisingly close. Nile felt the woman had warmth that was clearly evident in spite of her no-nonsense personality.

Of course, much of Moira's closeness to Nile had to do with the fact that she; like her husband, believed the young man they adored had found a woman who matched his own soft-spoken, reserved yet easily passionate demeanor. Moira saw a sadness-a slight…shame in Nile's eyes that almost mirrored Taurus'. It was as if they each carried the weight of the world on their shoulders. It was a weight neither deserved to bear.

Moira was setting the big pot to slow cook for two additional hours.

"Who's that man outside with Taurus?" Nile called out from where she stood near the double glass doors at the rear of the kitchen. "I don't think I've met him yet."

Moira angled her head to see and then smiled. "No I'm sure you'd certainly recall meeting Kraven DeBurgh."

"Ah…so that's him." Nile noted easing her hands into the back pockets of her jeans. "Incredible name," she added.

Moira was stirring her soup. "Incredible name for an incredible man," the melodic lilt of her voice tinged with devilment. "One wonders if the rest of him is as incredible as that face of his."

"Miss Moira!" Nile cried whipping round her head to gawk at the woman.

"Oh…" Moira scoffed with a flip wave. "Us old married girls can look just as closely as you young single ones."

Nile shook her head and turned back to the door. "Well who is he?"

"Close as a brother to Taurus." Moira shared, while setting a heavy lid in place atop the pot. "They began as…uneasy business associates and then became powerful allies almost from the moment they met face to face."

"Why *uneasy?*" Nile asked, tailing her fingers along her jaw as she continued to study the men.

Moira wiped her hands to her apron and smiled. "That's another story, my girl. But suffice it to say-the nature of Kraven DeBurgh's business is known to be no less than  mysterious at best."

"Mysterious as in illegal?" Nile probed.

"Mysterious as in if he told you he'd have to kill you." Moira explained and calmly went about her business.

Nile stared after her with wide eyes and an open mouth.

"I'll try not to feel too offended that everyone else in the borough has seen her while I, your dearest friend, haven't even been invited over for tea."

Taurus chuckled. "Are you done yet?" He asked the man pacing the grounds.

Kraven DeBurgh shrugged. "You could've at least let me see her-make sure she's worthy of you."

"Worthy hmm?"

Kraven's fiercely vibrant green gaze narrowed sinfully. "Bollocks, right?"

"Complete and utter bollocks," Taurus confirmed.

"So what's going on then?" Kraven inquired his voice and expression turning serious. "In all these years you've never brought a woman here. As *I* have first hand knowledge of all the beauties that traipse in and out of your life, I have to ask what it is about this one?"

Taurus hid his hands in his jean pockets and looked down. "At first I was simply blown away by her looks," he admitted slanting Kraven a wink when he laughed. "I wanted her in my bed but I tried not to be so obvious about it when we did the conversation thing." He reminisced with a smile. "We did the conversation thing for three hours that first night. When we finally got around to going to bed together, it was incredible but just another part of it all." He folded his arms across the hunter green sweatshirt he wore. "Sex had gone from being the *only* thing I wanted to being one of the many things I wanted from her." A muscle tightened along his jaw then. "She's trying to get me to accept that sex is all it was and all it could ever be."

"And you really don't believe that?" Kraven tilted his head to study his friend more closely. "Could it be that she's so beautiful and the sex was so lovely that you've got yourself thinking there's more?"

"I thought about that," Taurus tapped his index finger to the cleft in his chin. "But we had a week together and spent two days of it in bed. I wanted to know her...no Krave, it's about a lot more."

"And now you've got her here to...what? Convince her? Get her to come 'round to your way of thinking?"

Taurus shrugged. "She's already in love with me. She's just not sure she can trust me." He leaned against the trunk of a massive tree. "She's holding something back-something horrible for her. Maybe she thinks I won't feel the same once I hear it."

"How do you know that you would?" Kraven asked, resting against the other side of the trunk.

Taurus could only shake his head.

The silence was enough for Kraven, "A bit of advice mate, enjoy this time, enjoy her and let her come to you."

Taurus pushed off the tree and walked around to face his friend. "What about you? Could you be so patient if you knew the woman you loved was keeping something from you?"

Kraven's grin was devilment personified and he narrowed his eyes. "See, that's where we differ my friend. I'm far too gorgeous and persuasive," he declared resting a hand flat against the front of the cotton sweatshirt emblazoned with the name of his favorite hockey team. "My woman would never be able to resist telling me her life's story and secrets the minute I ask her."

Laughing, Taurus relished his friend's ability to push all cares to the fringe. The two of them shared a hearty hug and then Kraven clapped a hand to Taurus' shoulder.

"Let's go meet your lass, eh?" He decided with a sly wink.

# CHAPTER TEN

The next several days were filled with as much wonder as the previous ones. Nile knew the trip would soon reach its end, but for now she would content herself with what was. What-in a perfect world-could be.

She'd taken to having her morning coffee out on her favorite hillside. She stood there enjoying the serene overcast and fog-capped view that morning when she felt Taurus behind her.

He pulled her back against his chest slipping his arms about her and making her feel even cozier beneath the folds of her beige cashmere robe.

"You done?" he asked once she was sealed next to him.

She nodded, allowing him to take her coffee mug. He set it at their feet and then turned her to him. The moment she saw his face, Nile knew something was wrong.

"I owe you an apology." He said, smoothing his hands along her arms.

Nile could only watch him in confusion.

"I haven't been very careful with you."

"What? What do you mean?"

"Back in Montenegro," he twisted the belt of her robe between his fingers. "And here…"

She stepped closer, patting her hands against the denim shirt he wore outside dark carpenter's jeans. "Taurus what are you saying?"

He cleared his throat and looked uneasy. "We've been here enjoying each other-a lot of um spur of the moment… a lot of times we haven't used… protection."

The expectant look in Nile's dark eyes began to gleam with understanding. She managed a smile. "If it helps to know, I'm tested each year." She shrugged. "It's important for my older kids to see that sort of responsibility for one's health."

"I understand." He whispered. "I'm tested regularly myself," he shared with a gallant nod. "But that's not the only concern I have."

The expectant look returned to Nile's face.

"You could get pregnant this way." He informed her softly.

Nile felt her entire body weaken and wished she was sitting on the ground with her empty coffee mug. "Oh…" was all she could muster.

"Have I upset you?"

Nile could only shake her head.

Again, Taurus smoothed his hands across her arms. "It's just that I know there's something weighing on you. I can sense it even when we're having the best time together. I'm trying not to press you about it but I thought I'd speak on it hoping this might be the problem even though I don't really believe it is."

"You don't have to worry." She kept her eyes downcast. "You don't have to worry about getting me pregnant."

Taurus' fair features hardened with instant regret. He raged silently for once more saying the wrong thing.

"Hungry?" He asked then, stepping close to press a quick kiss to her forehead. "I'll get us some breakfast," he decided and set off before she could say anything.

Nile watched him go. She waited until he'd ventured down the hill before she tilted back her head and allowed a tear to slide from the corner of her eye.

♦　♦　♦

"Wow," Mick noted while she and Melina studied plates of Nile Becquois' work. "This'll certainly guarantee you a full house."

"Damn right it would." Mel toyed with the half moon that dangled from her earring. "I've tried before to get her for events at Crane's other galleries but it's real hard considering she doesn't do many showings. I wouldn't even be thinking of having an exhibit now if it wasn't for Dena. She and Taurus just took in a show of hers in Montenegro." She leaned over the table to shuffle through more of the plates. "The proceeds went towards the art studio she runs for kids in L.A. Maybe we could get her to come out for a charity event. I know Quest and Quay haven't decided on this year's cause." She gave a one-shoulder shrug. "Maybe you could run it by Q if you think it's got merit."

The mention of her husband's name brought a grimace to Mick's face. "No, no sure Mel I'll-I'll talk to him. It's a great idea."

Melina chewed her lip and debated before speaking. "I um…I noticed you and Quest were barely talking when he was in here earlier with Yohan."

Michaela seemed to wilt and hunched over the desk.

"Sweetie what is it?" Mel asked.

"Quest and Fernando stomped down the book. I have a feeling it's a done deal this time." She buried her face in her hands and groaned. "I haven't been speaking to him and I don't think he even has a clue about how angry I am. He's acting like it's nothing-like he's amused by it all, like it's a game to see how long I can take his taunts before I break down and beg him for sex."

Mel sat perched on the edge of the desk. "Well he *is* a Ramsey Mick. They thrive on sexual attraction, power…sometimes aggression. It's what makes them all so infuriating and sexy and so damned adorable." She said and rolled her eyes.

Mick slammed her fists to the table. "It isn't about that, dammit!"

"Well what then?" Mel snapped, frightened by Michaela's strange mood. "What's wrong?"

"What's wrong is I'm losing myself."

"Losing yourself-"

"A part of my…I don't know…my essence-the part that makes me who I am," she combed shaking fingers through her curls. "The part of me I felt I had to become." She confided, not resisting when Mel made her sit on the edge of the desk. "I feel like I'm losing my strength because Quest is so…*Quest*-the man who handles things, takes care of it all-takes care of everyone."

"He loves you and you love him." Mel said pulling curls from the collar of Mick's sweater.

"And that just gives him all the reason in the world to keep right on doing things his way."

"*And* he fell for you because you weren't a woman who'd allow him to do that. You remind him of that."

Mick smiled and nudged her elbow in Mel's side. "Sounds good, but I've got no idea what words to use. For once in my life, I don't know what the hell to say."

Mel shrugged and folded her arms across her gray suit coat. "Sometimes the way isn't always in the saying but in the doing."

A tiny buzz interrupted the moment.

"'Scuse me," Mel whispered moving to take the call from her assistant. "Yeah?… Yeah, yeah alright give me a sec. Mick? Sweetie, I'll be right back." She said before racing out of the office.

Alone, Michaela strolled over to the windows lining Melina's office. "Not in the saying but in the doing," she murmured and then nodded and reached for her cell. "County," she called once the connection was made. "It's Mick-call me when you get this message. It's time to stop screwin' around and get *"Royal Ramsey"* on the shelves."

◆　　◆　　◆

Nile's chocolate spiked heels echoed in the massive entryway as she rushed down the wide stone steps on her way to answer the bell. She was checking the backs of the gold studs adorning her ears while pulling open the door to Kraven DeBurgh.

"Kraven," she greeted breathless, smiling and silently pitying the woman who would capture the man's heart. Though that woman would be a lucky girl, she'd be doomed to life with a man she'd never be able to resist. That was quite a weapon for a man to have-an enjoyable weapon but a weapon just the same.

Kraven stepped past the door and peeked across Nile's shoulder. "Is he near?"

Nile glanced down the hall. "Just in the den."

"Well then," Kraven decided and leaned down to kiss Nile's cheek and joining in when she laughed. "I've been looking forward to this all week." He told her.

Nile easiness faded somewhat. "I can't say I've felt the same." She confessed and noticed the hurt shadow Kraven's handsome face. "I can't wait to have dinner together but…it's just knowing everyone will be there observing-judging…it makes me nervous."

"Ah," Kraven sighed and pulled her close. "The people here are some of the finest I've known," he smoothed her arms bared by the chic jersey dress she wore. "They're only curious. Everyone here loves T like a brother or son or…future husband." He winked and earned a shove in the side from Nile. "They only want to meet the love of his life." He went on and pretended not to notice Nile's stunned expression. His grin was as devilish as the glint in his jade stare. "If they haven't run *me* out of town, *you've* got nothing to worry about."

Nile tugged on the lapel of his salt and pepper suit coat. "Miss Moira said that you were involved in an… *uneasy business.*"

Kraven's laughter was full and deep when it echoed down the hall. "Ah Miss Moira…talk about curious. I believe they'd all give their finest properties to know what my *uneasy business* really is."

Nile squeezed her hand more tightly about his arm. "I'm not so sure about that. According to Miss Moira, you could tell us but then you'd have to kill us."

Again, the full deep of Kraven's laughter resounded through the corridor. They entered the den to find Taurus frowning fiercely as he stood near the fire. He was battling with a pair of silver cuff links. Nile just barely smothered her gasp when she saw him. Talk about being doomed to loving a man you couldn't resist, she thought. She wondered if he had a clue of how lost she was over him.

At Kraven's bellow, Taurus grinned and met him in the middle of the room for handshakes and hugs.

"I'm just going to finish getting ready guys," Nile left the two friends staring after her.

"Jesus," Kraven breathed, "how'd a fool like you find an angel like that?"

Taurus shrugged. "I guess after a lifetime of hell, God finally saw fit to smile down on me." He pondered, smiling when the cuff link snapped into place.

"If we could all be so blessed," Kraven breathed.

Taurus did a double take. "What's this? The die hard Casanova speaking wishes of monogamous love at long last?" he teased.

Kraven remained serious. "Only if I was blessed with an angel like that and I'm afraid God doesn't see fit to reward monsters such as myself with angels."

Taurus fixed his friend with a deep set stare that was both stern and honest. "I know monsters. I see none here." He clapped Kraven's shoulder before they shared a hug.

The Baird Pub was a rustic looking two story establishment located right in the heart of the borough. For its rustic appearance, however, the interior shrieked charm and elegance. The Irish proprietors Reese and Margret Baird decided; when they opened the business, that Invernesshire had enough rough and tumble dives and needed something that gave their simple environment a bit of posh.

This night, however, the Bairds put on even more of a gloss. After all, it wasn't every night the notorious and intriguing Kraven DeBurgh and; his equally intriguing and undeniably gorgeous chum Taurus Ramsey dined out. Word had already spread that the two men would be escorting Taurus' lady friend. The two story restaurant was filled with so many patrons-some had to be turned away.

"Still got a table for us Lou?" Kraven asked Lucas Morrisey the pub's host.

Lucas grinned checking his bow-tie while stepping from behind the podium. "I swear some of these blokes took their first baths of the season to dine here tonight." He winked and slapped three menus against Kraven's arm. "This may be an even bigger event than that ball of yours next week, eh?"

Kraven smirked. "Funny Lou," he knew the success of the ball would mirror the support he'd have for his plans to construct his hunting lodge near Stuart Castle.

Conversation in the golden-lit pub quieted a bit as Lou escorted the newly arrived guests to their table. Beauty radiated from the trio like sunrays but they wore it with an easy grace. Nile didn't feel as on edge as she'd expected. There were warm smiles and nods directed her way from every angle. Still, she wanted to give a nervous tug upon the twist front of her stunning chocolate frock. Instead, she gripped Taurus' and Kraven's arms a bit more tightly as they ventured deeper into the cozy dining hall. Gradually, conversation returned to its previous volume as the crowd settled in to eat and observe.

"I have absolutely no idea what to order." Nile admitted, her wide dark eyes focusing helplessly upon the menu.

"May I?" Kraven pressed a hand to the front of his salt and pepper double breasted suit coat.

"Oui," she replied gratefully and smiled.

Kraven sent her a wink and then seemed to recall that his best friend was sitting to his right. "I'm sorry T unless you'd like to-"

"No, no by all means." Taurus urged with a wave, knowing how seriously the man took the enjoyment of cuisine. Of course Kraven's obvious attempts to show off his ordering skills had Taurus rolling his eyes in boredom.

"So tell me about this ball you're having?" Nile asked once Kraven had placed the order for Scotch broth and Smoked Salmon with neeps and tatties. Entranced, she listened to him discuss his plans for the hunting lodge.

"Are you truly settled on life as a humble proprietor after living a life dealing in *uneasy business*?" She teased.

Kraven nodded but couldn't hide the smile from the lush curve of his mouth. "I've had enough of it Nile. I only hope the townspeople believe me."

"But they're good people. Best you've ever known, right?"

Kraven grinned acknowledging her reference to his earlier comment. "It's true," he took a sip of his Guinness. "But too much of my presence tends to set them on edge."

Nile could see that he was hurt by the fact in spite of the playful wink he sent her way.

Across the table, Taurus kept out of the conversation and took the chance to observe Nile. He wondered what her reaction would be should he tell her he loved her. What if she didn't reciprocate? What would *his* reaction be? Whatever the outcome, one thing was certain: she was his and his she would remain.

"That will certainly keep me full for a week." Nile shared complimenting the feast they'd just consumed. "I've got no room for the dessert you ordered," she sighed.

"Nonsense," Kraven said while signaling the waiter for a refill on beer. "The meal isn't complete without it and I think you'll come to love Clootie Dumpling as much as I do."

Nile laughed easily thinking if the name were any indication she wasn't so sure she'd share Kraven's sentiments. Her gaze drifted toward Taurus who'd been strangely quiet during dinner. His focused expression would've kept her heart wedged in her throat had it not been for Kraven's presence.

During the lull in conversation, Moira Bradenton stopped by the table to speak and asked Nile to meet some of her friends.

"Oh not you too Miss Moira?" Taurus teased, folding his arms over the front of the amber colored suit coat that enhanced the champagne allure of his eyes. "You're not getting caught up in all this hype, are you?"

"Can't be," Kraven joined in, "you can see us whenever you like Miss Moira."

Moira only rolled her eyes toward the two grinning gods. "Don't remind me," she told them. "Come love," she urged Nile and took her hand to escort her on into the enveloping crowd.

Kraven slanted a glance at Taurus before taking another swig of his beer. "With all my heart mate, I pray you'll keep her always. I fear for your future if you don't."

At last Taurus looked away from Nile.

"No way will you ever look at another woman the way you look at her." Kraven clarified without being asked.

"Hmph-am I *that* bad?" Taurus asked while reaching for his mug of Killian's Red.

Kraven shook his head. "Worse, my friend."

"If I tell her how I feel I can't be sure how she'll take it."

"But you won't know that 'til you do, right?"

Taurus grimaced. "Maybe I'm not ready for reality to set in." He tilted back the mug almost emptying it. "Having her here is like a dream. I know all the drama in my family will be an issue for us." He shook his head. "I'm in no rush to get back to it."

"I'll tell you what you already know T, the sooner you deal with the reality, the sooner you can start livin' the dream."

With that, the two raised their mugs in silent toast.

# CHAPTER ELEVEN

"Shall I carry you?" Taurus offered playfully when he opened the passenger door of the Land Rover.

Nile stepped out gingerly and raised a hand when she wobbled and Taurus stepped close to assist. She did however settle for letting him hold her hand when she wobbled a second time.

"It should be illegal to serve that much beer in a glass." She muttered.

Taurus shrugged and gathered her close. "It's Scotland people take their brew very seriously."

"Clearly *your* tolerance is near sky level."

Taurus smiled. "We Ramseys learn to drink at a young age."

Nile laughed while curving her fingers deeper into the butter soft fabric of his coat. "So you're saying it's a tradition passed from father to son, huh?"

The easiness in Taurus' light eyes faded then. "No room for that in my family."

Nile wasn't so tipsy that she didn't realize she'd said something wrong. She held her apology until they'd walked inside and were ascending the staircase.

"You don't have to apologize," he said once they'd stopped on the landing between her room and his own. "I'm the one who should be doing that."

"You?" Nile whispered leaning against the wall.

Taurus studied his thumb as he worked it in circles against his palm. "Remember that day I talked to you about not being more careful when we had sex?"

Nile closed her eyes. "Taurus...don't."

"I need to say this," he leaned against the wall as well. "I'm sorry if I gave you the idea that I'd be unhappy or upset if all this resulted in you having my child."

"Please," she managed as her voice had all but deserted her.

84

"Let me finish," he pleaded, his sleek brows drawn close in determination. "My father…my father was a real bastard-phony and pompous. His goal in life was to make my sister and me to be as perfect as he was foul. It was a shitty life and if it hadn't been for my mother who knows what sort of monster I would've become." He cleared his throat against a sudden rush of feeling. "I think what I want most is to prove I can be a better man-husband, father…than my own had been." Leaning full against the wall he rested his head back. "It's like a living thing in my gut-a chance to know my father hadn't passed his sickness, his twisted mentalities on to me…"

Nile's heart thundered in her ears when Taurus suddenly pulled her close. She looked everywhere but his face until he tilted his head and forced her to meet his gaze.

"I love you," he confessed in the rough perfection that was his voice. "I want to share your future-whatever terrors I see in your eyes that you feel you can't tell me. I want every part of you-good or bad and I pray you'll accept the same from me."

*God he doesn't know what he's saying,* Nile spoke silently even as her chest filled with emotion. It pained and overjoyed her to see the lost little boy expression on his face. His breathing was staggered as though confessing his feelings took everything from him. He wanted her confession, he deserved it. But what good would it do? What could she give him? Certainly not the chance to prove he could be a better father than Houston Ramsey. All she had to offer was a devastating story and the chance for him to feel more hatred than he'd ever known.

She wanted to wilt from the sorrow of it all. Somehow Taurus sensed it and moved closer brushing away her tears with the touch of his lips. His kisses trailed across her cheeks and then to her mouth. Nile tired of the teasing and instigated a deep kiss that surprised him enough to allow her to press him back to the wall.

She kissed him as if starved. "Mon Dieu…Je vous aime."

Hearing words of love on her lips, Taurus gripped her tightly and carried her effortlessly to his bedroom. Once the door had been kicked open, only the shuddery sounds of their breathing filled the dark.

Taurus kept her there against the door. He used his teeth and hands to strip away her dress. His mouth traveled the length of her body while he settled to his knees before her. Fluidly, he draped one of her legs across his shoulder.

Nile uttered something unintelligible when he began to feast upon the heart of her. She trembled fiercely and he pressed one hand to her stomach. The other gripped her thigh and kept her motionless as he pleasured her into orgasmic oblivion. Nile thrust helplessly against the length of his tongue using soft words of desire to beg him not to stop. Her words transformed into lilting cries that colored the black of the room.

When he finished, he pulled her high against him and let her kiss her taste from his tongue. Nile felt herself being lowered to the bed but as the room was terribly dark, her heart raced with need and uncertainty intertwined. She could feel him at her breasts-his hair like silk against her skin. He left no part of her untouched and spent ample time adoring her bosom. She moaned when he moved away, wanting him to continue suckling and nibbling.

He was gone but a few moments but then Nile felt him return. His lean chiseled form was warm and bare next to her and she raked her nails across his chest and back. Again, Taurus caught her thighs in his iron grip parting them for his body.

Nile shuddered when he took her. Granite hard, he throbbed inside the moist warmth of her love.

"You're not being careful again Mr. Ramsey," she teased though her words came out in a ramble of moans amidst the delicious thrusts that drove his length deeper.

"You're mine." Was his excuse. His softly rugged voice filled the room. "And I'm yours. Always," he vowed.

More words were unnecessary and undesired. He took her to the edge with the merciless drives of his sex. Then, with expert skill the heated drives tapered off to slow lunges that were no less stimulating. Nile could scarcely catch her breath. Taurus had captured both her wrists and imprisoned them above her head. He dipped his head to favor a nipple which he suckled as slowly as he rotated his stiffness inside her.

Nile was out of her mind with need. She rambled senseless words of delight in her native tongue which threatened to peak Taurus' pleasure sooner than he wanted. To silence her, he outlined her full lips with the tip of his index finger before slipping it inside her mouth. She suckled with an intensity that sent him erupting inside her and dropping his head to her shoulder. He cursed the loss of control while savoring the stunning satisfaction that gripped him.

♦    ♦    ♦

The manager's office door at Double Q was shut firmly behind Contessa's back. Her eyes shimmered with tears when she looked up at Fernando who scowled down at her.

"You get yourself together or we're leavin'. Do you understand me County?"

"I- I'm fine," she lied through a sniffle and wiped at her tears. "I'm fine," she tried once more.

"Liar," Fernando almost growled and brushed her hand away from her face. He did a far better job of removing the wetness from her cheeks and nose. "You're quiet as a mouse out there," he accused referring to the dining table where they enjoyed a couple's night out along with Quay, Ty, Quest, Mick, Yohan, Mel, Moses and Johari at the jazz club owned by the twins. "You being *that* quiet is a dead give away that somethin's wrong."

"Dammit why'd you tell me this?" she hissed pushing hard against his massive chest.

Fernando wasn't amused. "Because you wouldn't let me out of the damn house until I did."

"You could've lied."

"I've been doing that since I got back from that trip."

County sniffed. "What are you and Moses going to do?"

"Damned if I know," Fernando groaned, massaging his eyes in a weary manner. "We won't do a thing 'til Taurus gets back. Then we'll sit down with…we'll figure out something."

There was silence for a while and then County felt her tears back building and rubbed the flaring sleeve of her wrap blouse against her cheek.

"Hey shh…" Fernando urged, rocking County slow when her emotions got the best of her again. "Let me take you home?" he suggested, knowing she wouldn't be able to keep it together for the rest of the evening. He closed his eyes in relief when he felt her nod against his neck.

◆　◆　◆

Nile woke well before dawn that morning. Streams of light fought past the navy linen drapes and she realized they were the reason she couldn't see her hand before her face the night prior. No matter, because they'd added even more allure to the things Taurus Ramsey had done to her.

Still, it was the things he'd said that almost caused her heart to burst. She did love him and was certain the emotion was written all over her face. He was so good and he deserved so much more than the hurt and shame she would surely bring to the table.

Besides, she couldn't give him what he wanted most in the world. A child would never be in her future. While he professed to want every part of her-good and bad-she'd not suffer him to settle for a woman who couldn't give him the chance to prove he was a better man and shower love on a child of his own. Sorrow filled, Nile dragged herself from his bed and decided to bury her head under the covers of her own.

Taurus left his room shortly after Nile disappeared into hers. Something told him to give her space, so he bypassed her closed doors and headed downstairs. He took his coffee and enjoyed it while surveying the land. Then, he ventured out to the stone deck off from the kitchen. Smoothing a hand across his bare chest, he breathed in the morning air while staring off into the distance.

Gradually, the calm easy look he wore grew dark-sinister in its intensity. He turned, going to the dark pine set situated in the corner of the deck. Selecting one of the massive chairs, he smashed it against the stone fence surrounding the space. Having spent a portion of his rage, he dropped to one knee and squeezed his eyes shut to will his temper to cool.

◆　　◆　　◆

Nile paused at the entryway to the deck when she arrived there later that morning and noticed the crushed chair in the corner. Since it would've taken nothing less than a wrecking ball to destroy the heavy pine creation, she figured its demise was quite deliberate. The sound of her name in the distance interrupted her thoughts before she could dwell on them any longer.

"Nile?"

It was Kraven she realized. Looking across the stone expanse of the deck, she saw that he was seated at the round wrought iron table…along with Taurus.

Kraven was meeting her before she'd made it halfway to the table. "I was afraid I wouldn't have a chance to see you this morning." He pulled her into a tight hug. "Needed to find out if you're as incredible before noon as you are after hours." His striking green eyes gave her the once over. "Please to see that I've confirmed it."

Nile couldn't help but laugh, needing the release to flood away her tension. "Have you already eaten?" She asked once they'd approached the table and she saw the plates and silverware littering the surface.

"I'm sorry, love," he leaned close to kiss her cheek, "there were some things I needed to talk over with my mate here and now, with the ball preparations tugging at me every which way, I need to get moving."

"Could you use any help?" Nile asked, tugging at the wide sleeves of her gold lounging gown. She watched Kraven shake hands with Taurus-who had yet to acknowledge her and; whom she secretly suspected, was at fault for the broken chair. She hoped neither man could hear the desperation in her voice as she offered (begged) to help out with the festivities.

"No thank you, sweet," Kraven stole another kiss from Nile's cheek. "I'd adore it, but I've got a feeling my friend would kill me if I took you out of his sight."

Nile wouldn't dispute Kraven aloud though she doubted he'd have any problem taking her with him. One would have to be blind to miss the cold in Taurus's light stare.

Still, Kraven led her to the chair he'd just vacated. "I'll see you both later," he squeezed her shoulder, "you two have a nice chat." He said, scooting Nile's chair closer to the table while he sent his friend a meaningful look before he set off.

Alone, Nile struggled for some conversation spark. She was thankful Taurus wasn't watching her then which would've made thinking more difficult than it was already proving to be. Her eyes lilted on the broken chair.

"What happened to it?" She asked, nodding slightly in the direction.

Taurus, it seemed, was looking for his own 'out' and glanced toward the smashed chair as if he'd forgotten it. Suddenly, he pushed away from the table and stood. "Nothing I can't take care of," he said and then set off the deck without looking back.

♦     ♦     ♦

### Los Angeles, California~

"Are you sure?" Darby believed she finally understood what the phrase 'seventh heaven' meant as she marveled over the five canvases leaning against the far wall of her office. "These pieces…these pieces are exquisite." She said to the woman who'd come that evening bearing the breathtaking works. "I'm afraid I can't offer you much for them." She slanted the woman an uneasy look and pressed her lips together when she saw the statuesque lady raise a hand.

"I'd never take money for these." The woman's tilted brown gaze remained on the canvases as if she were entranced. "But you're right," she sighed, "they are exquisite and now they bring me nothing but pain when I look at them." She stepped close and leaned in to brush what may've been a bit of lint from the edge of the painting. "I can't see having them destroyed and my nephew has talked about your gallery so often since I've come to visit, that I can't think of a better place for them." Finally, she turned to Darby.

"And payment isn't necessary in light of all you and Ms. Becquois have done to give him and all the kids here a purpose- a future- a *good* future."

"Why…thank you," Darby whispered, truly moved by the beauty and touch of sadness in the woman's voice. She watched her gather the purse and wrap she'd arrived with before leaving as quietly as she'd arrived. The phone rang just as Darby realized the woman never told her who her nephew was.

Turning quickly, she rushed to answer the call before it went to voice mail.

"Darby hello."

Her questions about the mysterious benefactor ceased yet more filled her mind when she heard the rough, soothing voice in her ear.

"Taurus…" she eased into her desk chair, and then frowned. "Is Nile alright?"

"She's fine, she's fine." Sorrow for upsetting Darby caused Taurus' voice to soften. "Only I don't know how much longer I can interest her in staying."

"Oh um, I don't see how she could possibly be in any hurry to leave." Darby was conjuring an image of the man inside her mind.

Hearing the unspoken compliment, Taurus chuckled. "I appreciate you saying that, but I um, I'm afraid I haven't been the best host and I honestly don't want her to leave before I can get a grip on myself."

"How can I help?" Darby asked and felt her voice desert her when Taurus asked if he could fly her out to Scotland.

"Well I-oh Taurus I really don't think that's necessary. I could just as easily talk to Nile from here."

"I think it'd make her very happy to see you Darby. Everyone here is very sweet to her, but to see a familiar face…"

Darby could hear the desperation in the quiet rough of his voice and she sympathized. "You're really in love with her, aren't you?"

"I really love her. More than I ever thought I was capable of," he responded without hesitating. "Unfortunately, I don't think she really believes me and I need her to." His sigh mingled with a groan. "I'm pretty certain she'll want to leave when she sees you…but I didn't know what else to do except call you."

Darby drew a line through the remaining appointments on her calendar. "If you can give me a few days, I'll be there."

♦　　♦　　♦

"It looks grizzly, but it won't bit ya Miss."

Darby found her smile and even managed a nod before accepting Colin Bradenton's hand and leaving the car. She wasn't as afraid of being bitten as she was of being seriously underdressed when she arrived at the incredible manor house the following week. The appearance of the place made her feel as though she should be wearing a gown trailing past her feet instead of clunky hiking boots and sagging jeans.

"Is it as big on the inside?" she asked.

"Aye, that it is," Colin confirmed with a tip of his brown cap. "But my missus would swear it's three times bigger than that!"

Darby let out a whistle while staring up at the magnificent structure and then around the encompassing grounds.

"Just give it a good rap!" Colin instructed Darby as he unloaded her bags from the trunk.

Taking a deep breath, she gazed upon the wide door she stood before and grabbed onto the brass knocker. She smiled upon hearing her friend's distinctive voice.

"I have it Miss Moira!" Nile called while whipping open the door. She gasped looking as if she'd seen a ghost.

Darby winked. "Hope I won't cramp your style," she said.

Nile screamed and pulled her best friend close. "What are you doing here?" She squealed and kissed Darby's cheek.

"Taurus called," Darby offered a knowing smile. "He said he thought you might want me here."

Nile could only nod and pull her friend into another hug.

The scream and subsequent squealing brought the other three people in the house rushing into the entryway.

"It's alright." Nile said to ease the worry on their faces.

"Thanks for coming." Taurus clasped one of Darby's hands into both of his.

"No problem." Darby's voice sounded uncharacteristically hushed as she took note of the fierce looking man standing off from the group. She managed to stop gawking in time to greet the woman who stood close to Nile.

"Moira Bradenton. I trust my husband didn't drive too outrageously on the way out here?"

"Oh-oh no. The drive was just fine." Darby said with laughter filling her words as she shook hands with Moira. Her ease tapered off a bit then when she saw Taurus drawing the man close.

"Darby Ellis, my good friend Kraven DeBurgh."

Again, Darby tried not to gawk which was virtually impossible given the man's dark incredible looks. She cast a quick glance at Nile; who smiled knowingly. Nodding, Darby extended her hand toward Kraven. "Nice to meet you," she said and was thankful that her voice didn't waver.

Subdued wasn't a term one would use in reference to Kraven DeBurgh. Subdued however, was a perfect description of his manner. "I trust you'll enjoy your stay Ms. Ellis."

"Thank you."

Taurus' face held the same knowing smile as Nile's. He stepped forward and clapped Kraven's back. "Let's give these two some time to talk." He suggested.

Alone, Nile and Darby hugged again and tried to catch up in the span of a few moments. Nile told Darby that everyone was rushing to and fro in preparation for that evening's ball. Of course, Nile was most interested in hearing about her kids. Darby was pleased to announce that it was business as usual-the studio was in the very capable hands of the staff.

"Word spread very quickly about the Montenegro event," Darby shared folding her arms across the scoop neckline of her gray Henley sweater. "The studio's been flooded with requests for shows."

Nile shrugged and tucked a lock of hair behind her ear. "Well that's pretty standard after I've put on a show, you know?"

"Mmm but rarely are we invited to take part in charitable events with corporate giants like the Ramseys."

Nile's expression signaled the request for more info. Darby filled in the details as they ascended the staircase in route to a guest room. When Nile seemed to seriously consider the idea of an event sponsored by the Ramseys, Darby allowed her happy surprise to show.

"Not only is Taurus Ramsey gorgeous as a god, but he's got the unique power to convince you without even asking."

"Please," Nile rolled her eyes toward the tapestries lining the walls, "it's got nothing to do with him. The Ramseys are well known for their devotion to these causes. Since their interests surround the welfare of children, I don't see how I can say no."

"Of course," Darby conceded with a curtsy.

Nile's responding wave was comical enough but Darby could sense her friend needed her very much.

"Alright look, why don't you sit down and tell me why Taurus felt he had to call and get me out here?" Darby was asking once she'd gotten past the momentary shock over her stunning room. "And please don't tell me that you don't know," she interjected while tightening the barrette that held her curls in a high ponytail. "I could see it on your face when you opened the door."

"He wants me," Nile admitted, toying with the fringe hem of her mauve sweater. "He wants all of me. Wants me to be his wife, have his kids…"

Darby sat on the bed and let her legs dangle over the low cherry wood footboard. "Honey how do you feel about him really? I mean…" her green eyes sparkled as they looked out over the room, "he's almost unreal-physically." She shrugged. "Is it only about his looks? Skills in bed?" She asked in a softer voice while leaning back to brace herself on her elbows.

Smiling, Nile shook her head and took no offense to her friend's questions. "It should be about that." She laughed shortly. "Mon Dieu, it'd make things so much easier…" She fixed Darby with a resigned look. "It's not though, it's not. There's so much more- so very much more…I love him so."

Glee added a deeper glow to the rich honey tone of Darby's face. "Thank God, because the man is completely gone over you." She breathed her elation. "And you should be thrilled! It's clear as day that you two are fools for each other."

Nile's laugh was short…humorless. "Right and a fool is just what he'll believe I've taken him for when he finds out who I am."

"You know, you never really told me the full story." Darby recalled and set aside her overnight case to give herself more room on the spacious bed. "Now, here in this perfect place seems like a perfect time, don't you think?"

Nile nodded accepting that the time had come long ago and her friend deserved to know it all-consequences be damned. "Well you know all about France," she groaned, leaning back in one of the mocha suede armchairs flanking the fireplace. "And about my real mother passing away…I spent a couple of years being raised by my grandmother. Then one day my father shows up," she shrugged, "I was about seven and happy enough to see him I guess. He always brought me pretty good presents. But the visits were always brief and I'd gotten used to it. I think I preferred it. But on this particular day he tells me I'm coming to live with him. True childhood after that was a distant memory."

Nile noticed Darby flinch and shook her head. "He didn't touch me. There were too many other little girls around for him and his sick friends to take their pick of." Leaning forward, she buried her face in her hands and inhaled before looking up. "Remember all that press with the Ramseys and their connection to a man named Cufi Muhammad?"

Darby's expression reflected knowing just as Nile announced that Cufi Muhammad was her father.

"Now what's Taurus supposed to think of me when I tell him that? The fact that I tried to get every branch of the law to believe what I had to say and failed, won't matter a bit once he finds out what I came from."

"That's got nothing to do with you."

"Right D," Nile sighed and massaged her neck. "That might play out if my father were a jewel thief or evil scientist but this is a man who kidnapped, sold and exploited children for profit."

"Fair enough," Darby agreed with a smirk. "But regardless of the fact that Taurus looks like an angel, I sense he's a good man. Something won't let me believe he'd hold you responsible for a thing like that."

"Not knowing for certain is why I can't tell him. He looks at me like-like I'm the best thing…like he's seen beneath the meaningless surface appeal to who I really am-who I could be if I didn't have the blood of a monster."

"Shit Nile," Darby left the bed then. "Taurus sees what everyone else sees. The only person who can't see the good in you is *you* and baby no one-not Taurus, not me, not even the kids can make that happen." She knelt before Nile's chair and gave her a shake. "I think we can help though. I don't think shutting us out or shutting out Taurus is the answer. I don't want to see you hurting anymore than you are now and I think pushing that man away would do just that."

Nile smoothed her hands across Darby's where they'd come to rest on her knees. "Odds are he'll find out soon enough."

"Then tell him dammit! Tell him before it comes out another way-which may very well have him thinking that you hid it because you *are* in league with your father. Oh honey," Darby pulled Nile close when her eyes grew impossibly wide. "The things he said to me on the phone-his feelings for you...he loves you so deeply I'm surprised he can stand beneath the weight of it. Tell him. I don't think you'd be sorry."

Nile kissed Darby's forehead and then leaned back in the chair and fixed her with a look of amused doubt. "Why don't you save that prediction until I tell you the rest?"

# CHAPTER TWELVE

"Wow! And I thought *I* put in some long hours."

Moses turned away from locking the door to his building and found himself staring at Michaela who leaned against the passenger side of his Hummer.

Hissing a curse, he bolted toward her. "What are you doin' on this end of town at this time of day?" He demanded, glancing around the deserted street. "Q with you?"

Mick grimaced. "I waited 'til after hours so I wouldn't run into anyone."

"What the hell are you doing here?" He pushed open the building door and pulled her inside Ramsey Bounty.

"I need your help," she told him simply once they stood in the front office. "You're the only person I know who's as good as or better at this than I am."

Moses set Mick to one of the cushioned chairs in the lobby's living area. "And what exactly is *this*?" He asked while leaning against the receptionist's desk.

Mick rubbed clammy hands across her jean clad thighs. "I need you to find someone or as much about them as you can. I've done my best and I'm against a brick wall now-a brick wall I'm assuming would take the expertise of someone with your skills to break through."

"What's this about Mick?" Moses' voice was low, his frown deep as he watched her reach into a jacket pocket. "Charlton Browning?" he read the name off the folded sheet of paper she passed him. "Who is he?"

Mick pressed her lips together and turned to face him more fully. "Before I tell you, I want you to promise me something."

Moses remained silent.

She lowered her eyes and continued. "Don't tell Quest you're doing this."

"Mick-"

"Moses please!"

"Hell Mick what is this about? You tell me everything here. Now."

"Moses please-please just help me here, alright?!" She shuddered once and broke down into a desperate cry that seemed to shock her as much as it did Moses. "Damn tears," she grumbled and rubbed at her eyes.

"Jesus," Moses whispered, leaving the desk to pull her close. "I promise, alright? I won't say a thing but you're scaring me here."

"Sorry," she managed with a shaky nod.

Moses cupped her chin and made her look at him. "Save the apologies and tell me everything."

◆　　◆　　◆

"I don't know about this." Nile said watching skeptically as her hair was pulled up and back away from her face.

"Give it a rest," Darby argued and continued securing the elaborate array of pin curls about the high chignon she'd styled. "You keep it in your face enough and this is a special occasion-a ball with the man you love. Hell, how dreamy is that?!"

"Yeah…"

"What are you gonna do?" Darby asked, taking note of the unease still clinging to her friend's voice.

Nile met Darby's gaze in the mirror. "I'm going to enjoy the ball and then head back with you to L.A. You don't agree?" She asked, noticing the way her friend's face changed in the mirror.

Darby shook her head. "I still think you should tell him everything."

"Even after I told you the rest?"

"*Especially* because of the rest," she emphasized and propped a fist to her hip. "Have you forgotten about all the powerful men Taurus knows? Surely they-"

"Wouldn't lift a finger to stop this. Many of those *powerful* men were also clients of my fathers. You don't know how long…how many times I tried. Finally I had to accept the fact that those *authority figures* were as corrupt as the rest…" Nile shook off the agitation of it all and put happiness in place. "I wish you'd come with us tonight."

Satisfied with the lovely chignon, Darby moved from behind Nile and headed to the closet. "So sorry but I forgot to pack my steamer trunk full of elaborate evening gowns."

"Oh please, I'm sure there's something in all that stuff Taurus bought me."

"Yes love, but how ever would it fit across all this?" She teased and waved toward the ample bosom that outsized her friend.

"Show off," Nile hissed following Darby to the closet where she pulled her into another hug. "Thanks girl."

96

"Anytime," Darby sighed, rubbing Nile's back before setting her away. "Alright, enough of this sappy stuff. Let's get you dressed."

Twenty minutes later, Darby marveled over her best friend. The ball gown was the stuff of princesses with its train following gracefully. The gown itself was a gorgeous champagne satin creation with a blazer style bodice and up-turned collar that emphasized the elaborate style of Nile's hair and the dangling gold earrings that glimmered against the light.

The two headed downstairs where Taurus waited. Of course, he was no less dashing in the almond brown tux he wore. The three quarter length jacket accentuated the stunning breadth of his back and shoulders while the color accentuated his fair skin, eyes and hair.

Darby urged the devastating couple to have fun and kept her smile in place until the door shut behind them. Alone then, Darby sat there on the huge stone steps and worried for her friend.

◆　　◆　　◆

Kraven DeBurgh's home was the manor house that stood on the vast acreage that had been in his family for centuries. The great castle that eclipsed it had been deserted ages ago, but had become the source of much conversation since Kraven's announcement that he wanted to turn it into a hunting lodge. Kraven met with as much opposition from the townspeople as he did from members of his own family. They had no wish to see their land overrun with overzealous tourists and their guns. Not to mention the many *unsavory* elements from Kraven's past. In their opinion, it was simply Kraven's way of appeasing the blood lust that had fueled his actions since boyhood.

Though he had his own money and the support of the authorities, Kraven knew that without the town's blessing, such an endeavor would be dead in the water. The ball that evening was an attempt to woo and there were few who could resist Kraven DeBurgh when he was in a wooing mood.

Nile stood staring around the great hall of Kraven's home feeling much the same way she had the first time she'd set eyes on the home Taurus kept a few miles away. Kraven's home was made more elaborate amidst the gala décor.

"Glad you came?" Taurus asked, leaning down to kiss her cheek when she nodded like a gleeful school girl. Before Nile could completely lose herself in the captivating atmosphere, she and Taurus were surrounded and being greeted by residents of the borough.

"Incredible," Kraven complimented when he set eyes on Nile in her gown. "And where's our Ms. Ellis?" He inquired as he looked toward the entryway.

Nile appeared down for the first time since she'd arrived. "I couldn't get her to come-said she didn't have a thing to wear."

"Nonsense," Kraven breathed without realizing how clearly the disappointment was etched on his face.

"So how are things going?" Taurus asked hoping to lighten his friend's mood. "You winning 'em over?"

"Well," Kraven sighed while glancing about at his guests. "I believe they've been feeling more charitable towards me lately. Perhaps it's the company I'm keeping." He said and leaned down to kiss Nile on the mouth.

"Hey, hey you got *her* sold," Taurus pulled Nile against him. "Back to your guests, Lord DeBurgh."

Kraven chuckled and slapped the back of Taurus' head before disappearing into the crowd.

Later, Nile and Taurus ventured upstairs where the second dance floor was located. There, the music changed from the more classical style that filled the lower level, to something a bit more provocative. They barely moved to the easy tempo.

Taurus' expression was steady and unwavering as he held Nile. She wondered if he could feel her heart thudding against the bodice of her gown.

"Thank you Taurus," she said once a few moments of silence had passed between them.

He tilted his head. "What for?"

"Darby. She told me that you thought I might need her."

"Was I right?"

Nile focused on the satiny mocha tie where it disappeared inside his stylish jacket. Taurus caught her neck in his hand and made her look up at him.

"When Darby leaves in a few days, I-I'm going with her." She whispered in a rushed, panicky tone.

Taurus' gaze followed the line of his thumb where it trailed her cheek. "I figured on that when I decided to call her."

"So you're not angry?"

"I'm past angry," he admitted the muscle jumping along his jaw was proof. "But forcing you to stay doesn't appeal to me just now."

Nile studied a gold chandelier glistening in a far corner while summoning courage to ask her next question. "Are you finally agreeing that it won't work between us?"

He set his thumb beneath her chin then. "I'll never agree with that but I've got no problem giving you time to reconsider things."

She clasped her hands against his chest. "And if I don't...reconsider?"

He gathered her close and looked out over the sea of slow-dancing bodies. "Then I guess the next time I'll just have to keep you until I change your mind."

"Taurus-"

"I don't want to talk about this anymore, alright?"

Nile barely had the chance to nod before he was kissing her powerfully, hungrily and without care for whoever may've been watching. Nile clung to him, wishing they were alone but savoring the time they had for such sweetness. The kiss went on, intensifying and outlasting the melody that drifted overhead.

"Lord DeBurgh?"

Kraven grinned and shook his head when he heard the summons. He knew it'd make no sense to ask Seamus Hale- the caretaker who tonight was doubling as butler- to drop the title and use something…less stately. Alas, Seamus was a true member of the old school and would stick to formalities until his dying day.

Instead of answering to the ostentatious tag, Kraven simply bowed his head.

Seamus bowed as well. "A call for you, Sir."

Any lightheartedness Kraven had been feeling over the success of the event, fled when he heard the low gruff voice on the other end of the line.

"Haven't we come a long way, *Lord DeBurgh*?"

Instinctively, Kraven cast a glance across his shoulder. "Hill."

"I heard you were trying to revamp your family home." Hilliam Tesano's laughter was a long standing accompaniment to his words. "It's good to hear Krave. I know how long you've wanted to leave our ugly lifestyle behind."

"Mmm…and have you done the same?"

Hill laughed outright that time. He sounded as if he had no better chance of that happening than of hell freezing over.

"Why have you called Hill?" Kraven tired of the brief walk down memory lane.

"You heard about the goings on of Cufi Muhammad."

Intrigued now, Kraven kicked his study door shut. "Get to the point."

"There's talk of a cleanup project."

Kraven's heart sank, followed by him sinking into the nearest chair. 'Clean up project' had only one meaning in their world and it was nowhere near honorable. "Who?" He growled.

"The lovely ladies- *children*," Hill clarified with unmasked distaste coloring his voice then, "once under Mr. Muhammad's care."

"Jesus…when?"

"Once they're located."

Kraven realized his hand had numbed from the fist he'd clenched. "Can it be stopped?" He asked, hearing Hill sigh over the line.

"A few months ago, I'd have said 'not likely."

"And now?"

"Now? Well now things are being set in motion that could change that. I need to know if we can count on you when the tide turns?"

Kraven tugged at the bow tie that seemed to be choking him. He told himself he was done with all that. He wanted quiet now. He needed it.

"Krave?"

"Call me." He said and clicked off the phone.

◆　　◆　　◆

"You think it's all connected?" Carlos McPherson was asking Moses when they met for late drinks at the condo Carlos kept in Seattle.

"Can't be sure," Moses said and tilted back the rest of his whiskey grimacing at the satisfying burn working its way down his gullet. "Until we find out more I say it's best to keep our guard up all the way round."

Carlos focused on the pushups he made with his fingers. "How's Dena?" He asked.

Moses winked. "Don't you know?"

"I've been tryin' to give her space."

"Ah…right. Space. And how's that workin' out?"

"Not well."

"Then forget it," Moses stood to freshen his drink. "As long as she's here, you keep an eye on her. As close an eye as possible."

Carlos nodded. "I plan on doing just that."

◆　　◆　　◆

"Stop being such a fool, dammit!" Darby told herself just after another clash of thunder sent her screeching in terror. She was rocking back and forth on the living room sofa when the door knocker cracked and the sound echoed loudly. She jumped but took pride in the fact that she didn't scream.

Drawing strength from someplace deep she padded from the living room and down the corridor toward the front door. She prayed it might've been Nile and Taurus returning early from the ball. The last thing she expected was to open her door to the dark stranger she'd met earlier that afternoon.

"Mr. DeBurgh?" She queried softly.

Kraven grinned. "Ms. Ellis."

Before Darby could ask what he was doing there, another clash of thunder sounded. She screeched and jumped close to Kraven.

"Sorry," she murmured thoroughly embarrassed while looking down at her fingers curled around the lapels of his cloak.

Kraven was quiet for a moment, taking time to inhale the floral scent of her honey blonde curls. A wave of possessiveness surged through him so fast it might have been imagined. "Are you alright?" he managed to ask.

"What are you doing here?" Darby searched his entrancing green eyes with her own.

"I um…" *Jesus what's wrong with me?* He wondered and then glanced past her. "Could I come in first?"

Taking note of her manners, Darby eased her bruising grip on his clothes. "Please," she said and stepped back to allow him entrance. She watched him shrug out of the cloak but concern shuddered through her before her mouth could go dry at the sight of him in the tux. "Nile and Taurus?" she questioned moving close. "Are they alright?"

Kraven shook his head. "I'm sorry for making you worry. They're fine. I'm here to check on you."

Darby stepped back. "Check on me?"

"Nile wanted to leave when the storm started," he explained, "she was worried knowing how terrified you get."

Darby's lashes fluttered and she leaned against the wall in defeat.

"They were having such a good time, I volunteered to come instead."

"Good grief," Darby moaned wishing she could shrink beneath the folds of her pale blue terry robe and disappear. "Now I'm both sorry *and* embarrassed."

"You were also frightened," he reminded her coolly, "that outranks sorry and embarrassed *any* day."

"It's pathetic." She grumbled shoving her hands into the robe's pockets. "A stupid childhood fear I should've gotten over long ago. I'm thirty-two for heaven's sake."

Kraven's smile accentuated the lush curve of his mouth. "I'm thirty two as well and the sight of a spider still scares the living shite out of me."

Darby couldn't help but laugh when he shivered. The phrasing and accent were a truly amusing combination.

Kraven winced. "Sorry."

She shook her head. "It's funny to imagine someone like you being terrified of something so small."

Kraven would've loved to have known what she meant by *someone like him* but satisfied himself with believing it was something flattering.

"I'll make you a deal," he sighed and stepped closer. "If we see a spider *you* take care of it."

"Deal. And what do we do about my storm fear?"

Kraven offered his arm and winked when she accepted. "Talking always helps. If we find a good topic, the time could fly right by and the storm will be over."

"True," Darby agreed with a slow nod. "But the storm could go on for hours and aren't you busy bribing the townspeople at your ball?"

Kraven chuckled even as Darby tensed over her words.

"That sounded better in my head," she regretted, "I should've left it there."

His face held a look of playful surprise. "Why? That's precisely what I've been doing and it's worked beautifully so the rest of my night is free."

Tapping a finger to her chin, Darby pretended to be in heavy concentration. "I'll have to remember that a ball is the *real* way to win friends and impress enemies."

"That and having Nile Becquois in your corner," he cautioned. "Everyone loves her so," his devastating features softened. "The fact that she's my best friend's girl, gives me the edge."

Again, Darby nodded. "Yeah she's one of a kind."

Another crash sounded and she clutched Kraven's arm. The feel of his unyielding bicep beneath her fingers seemed to steady her somehow.

Kraven steered them into the den where he had her sit with him on the sofa.

"You're worried about her." He determined.

Darby wouldn't deny it. "Always," she admitted, "She's...so closed off about things she thinks no one would understand."

"Aye, that could be true for most of us," Kraven noted while unbuttoning his jacket and settling more comfortably on the sofa.

"Nile's one of the lucky ones though. She's got someone there to draw strength from-someone she can tell her secrets and fears." Darby dragged a hand through her curls. "I just don't want her to lose that."

Kraven hugged her close. "You needn't worry I seriously doubt my friend's going anywhere."

Darby closed her eyes, allowing herself to take comfort in the embrace. "She can be stubborn as an old mule. I can't count how many men she's sent packin' without a second thought."

Kraven gave her another squeeze. "Let's not forget love, my man's a Ramsey."

Laughter flowed between the two of them as the storm gradually subsided.

# *CHAPTER THIRTEEN*

They didn't head inside upon returning from the ball in the wee hours of the morning. Instead, Taurus drove to their favorite hillside and took in the arrival of daylight which broke to find them cuddled on a dry blanket atop the hood of the SUV . There, they silently observed the atmosphere and the emotion between them.

"I love you," Nile told him and snuggled back in his comforting embrace.

"You have all of my heart," he murmured into the top of her head. "But you won't stay," he knew.

"I can't."

"How do you know?"

There was silence for a while. Nile toyed with the cuff of his cream shirt and gathered her resolve. "All that's happening with your family...I'm so sorry. You need to take care of them- family's important. Sometimes it's hard to know if protecting them is worth all of the headache."

"No truer words have ever been spoken." Taurus agreed with a humorless chuckle. "I thank God that at least I know what to do to protect them this time. My father's...dead. What's left is to find and bring down my uncle and that son of a bitch Muhammad."

Nile bristled. "From what I hear he's a real monster."

"Bad as they come." Taurus confirmed. "But if we find the daughter, we'll have him in a heartbeat."

"Daughter? Do you believe she's...in contact with him?"

"At this point, who knows? But we're pretty sure she's the key-literally to bringing the man down."

"Sounds like a foolproof plan."

"Hmph. That would depend on the daughter. And whether she's a decent person or a twisted idiot like her father."

Nile closed her eyes while struggling to swallow past the lump of emotion in her throat. "You...you sound like you've made up your mind about her."

Taurus tightened his hold about Nile and set his chin into the crook of her neck. "My cousins think she'll cooperate. I'm not so sure-a woman lives a life like that influenced by an animal like that, we can't just assume none of it rubbed off."

Nile chose her next words carefully. "It doesn't have to be the case-regardless of what he was."

"She lived her life-much of her adult life watching her father peddle children. I've got no sympathy or benefit of the doubt for a woman like that." He said, ignoring the thoughts that said just the opposite. After all, his father was just that sort of man and he hadn't seen it-never even suspected. Besides, wasn't it vital to him that he not be judged because of Houston Ramsey's twisted needs? To cast this woman off as unworthy seemed beyond cruel.

Unfortunately, Taurus' silence told Nile just what she's suspected. He'd never understand and; ironically, her reluctance to tell him would only make it look like she was trying to protect her father and what was assumed to be her lifestyle. In truth, all she'd really wanted was to hold onto the man she loved just a little longer. What a mess she'd made of things.

Taurus snapped out of his own deep thoughts and took note of her shivers. "Let's get out of this morning air, hmm?"

Nile let him bundle her back into the SUV. She cast a long last look across the land knowing she might never see it again.

Darby inhaled deeply and woke with a start once the aroma of pine and an unfamiliar yet fabulously scented male cologne filled her nostrils. Blinking madly, she pushed a tumble of curls from her face only to have them fall back in her eyes when she realized who she'd fallen asleep upon.

"Kraven?" She blinked, checking to see if she was dreaming. She had her answer when his dreamy Scottish brogue touched her ears as he greeted her good morning.

"God," she moaned, closing her eyes when his opened.

Darby was so unnerved that she missed the completely *unnerving* manner in which Kraven studied her. He felt as though he'd been struck, but couldn't lock in on what had done it. Of course that was understandable since there was so much about her that had fascinated him in the few hours that he'd known her.

"What's your hurry?" He asked when she tried to ease off him.

"I'm so sorry," Darby looked as miserable as she sounded. "I never intended to keep you here all night because of my silly fears." She hissed.

"Please don't apologize to me again," his deep set greens traced her face in a manner that was almost hypnotic. "There was nowhere else I wanted to be. Please believe that."

"What about the ball?" Darby prayed the swell of emotion in her throat wouldn't choke her.

"Ah the ball," Kraven gave a playful wince while dragging a hand through the wavy black of his hair. "Well let me think, yes, yes…I recall they were laughing, drinking and had their main squeezes in hand when I left." He fixed her with an adorable lopsided grin. "I'd say it was a successful gathering, wouldn't you?"

Darby released some of her tension and laughed with him. Still, she couldn't help but take stock of their position; relaxed on the sofa where they'd fallen asleep while talking the night before. Awkwardly, she tried to tug close the lapels of her terry robe while pressing away from him.

"We should be moving. I wonder if Nile and Taurus are back?"

Kraven of course made no move to relinquish his comfortable spot on the sofa. His hand remained in its proprietary position on Darby's hip and kept her from venturing too far.

"With the storm, I hope they accepted my offer to stay the night." He snuggled deeper into the sofa and smiled contentedly as his eyes closed again. "I'm sure most everyone else stayed over."

"Well thank you so much for stopping by." She bit her lip and focused on her hands splayed across his chest. The crisp white shirt worn with the tux was partly unbuttoned and Darby blinked away from the sight of the bronze slab of chiseled muscle beneath. "Thank you for staying." She added when she realized he'd caught her staring.

Kraven gave into his needs and reached out to allow his fingers a dance across her brow. Silently, he wondered at the unease on her face. "One day, you'll have to tell me what sparked that fear."

Darby cleared her throat on the hint that there would be a 'one day' between them. "It uh…it isn't the happiest story."

He tugged on a curl. "Most stories about fears aren't, love."

Melting then, Darby let herself slide back into bliss when his hand delved into her hair and his fingers massaged her scalp. The key scraping the lock caught their attention and next they heard Taurus and Nile's hushed voices.

Darby sent Kraven an apologetic smile. "Thank you," she whispered and waited for him to ease his grip on her hip before she pushed herself away.

While everyone shared morning greetings out in the great hall, Kraven massaged his eyes and made no move to leave the sofa.

◆　　◆　　◆

105

Following the emotional scene with Nile earlier that morning, Taurus didn't think laughter would be anywhere within his realm of accomplishment that day. Still, he couldn't recall when he'd last laughed as hard as he had when Kraven told him during breakfast that he not only intended to turn the castle into one of Europe's premier hunting lodges but to devote time to cultivating the land.

Taurus would never affix the label 'Farmer' to his brooding friend. Kraven's confirmation of becoming just that had his eyes filling with tears of laughter.

"Alright now, seriously." Taurus gave another short laugh and wiped his eyes. "What in hell made you add this to your list of goals?"

Kraven shrugged, scratching at his chest beneath the billowing fabric of the mocha shirt he wore. "Not all together sure....I mean, for a long time I intended for the castle to be my main focus." He stood from the table and cast a guarded look across the rolling green of the never ending hills. "It'd be a welcome change after a lifetime of frustration." He trailed a thumb across his lips when they curved into a smile. "Then I meet Darby and..."

Taurus' amusement curbed as intrigue settled in. "Darby." Silence took hold while he added one more spoonful of sugar to his black coffee. "Love at first sight?" He eventually guessed.

Kraven cocked his head. "Cliché."

"It happens." Taurus grinned, thinking of Quest and Mick, himself and Nile...

"I don't rightly know T," Kraven turned to lean back against the stone wall enclosing the deck. "All I can be sure of is that I don't want her going back to L.A. Not yet..."

Taurus only nodded. He could very well understand that and thought of the woman he was trying to keep for a lifetime.

"Damn it all...what a fucking time to get a call from Hill."

Losing taste for his coffee, Taurus sat a little straighter. "Hill? Tesano?"

"One and only."

Taurus didn't need to ask why he'd called. He could read Kraven's expression all too clearly. Besides, his friend wouldn't talk about it in depth. He never had in spite of what he knew regarding Ramsey involvement with the Tesanos.

"Is there anything I need to know?" He had to ask.

"Not yet." Kraven slanted Taurus a meaningful look when he glanced across his shoulder.

◆   ◆   ◆

Kraven seemed to enjoy his job as host, for following breakfast that morning, he invited Taurus, Nile and Darby on an excursion that carried them into the Scottish Highlands.

Nile and Darby agreed that nothing in books or even with a tour group could compare to an authentic showing of the country by one of its own. Kraven had a story for everything and every place. It was past nightfall when the foursome returned to the castle.

"So I've been meaning to apologize."

Darby tucked a curl behind her ear and frowned at Nile. "Apologize?"

Nile kept her eyes on Kraven and Taurus who had walked on ahead. "About this morning. We didn't mean to interrupt." She glimpsed the bewilderment on her friend's face and giggled. "Oh please Darby, did you think we didn't notice you sharing the sofa with our charming, gorgeous host?"

Darby focused on tugging at a button on her denim jacket. "You're to blame for it. Just where do you get off embarrassing me like that? Sending a complete stranger to check and make sure I wasn't too afraid in the big bad storm."

Nile shrugged, kicking at a rock with the tip of her hiking boot. "Figured you wouldn't mind over much once he got here."

Fighting off the urge to smile, Darby nudged Nile's shoulder with hers. "I should kick you for even introducing me to a lovely thing like that when I've got to go back to Cali in a few days."

"You don't *have* to go back."

"But I do." Darby raised her brows in a mischievous gesture. "We got a huge donation just before Taurus called me out here. And besides," she smirked and shook her head, "No sense starting something that hasn't got a chance in hell of being about anything."

Nile muttered a curse. "People make long distance relationships work every day."

Darby eased hands into the back pockets of her jeans and watched Kraven and Taurus across the clearing. "Physical distance can manifest itself in many ways Ny." She smoothed the back of her hand across her honey brown cheek while voicing the statement.

"Darby..." Nile whispered, understanding then and pulling her friend into a tight hug.

Kraven enticed the group to share a glass of locally brewed brandy before heading back to Taurus' place. The moment was cozy and serene. Taurus and Nile sat cuddled before the fire. Kraven and Darby sat a ways off, both staring pensively into the fire and leaning forward just slightly with arms draped over their knees.

"It's an incredible thing you want to do here Kraven."

"Thanks," he downed a bit more brandy, "everyone thinks my having a hunting lodge is about some blood lust I'm trying to satisfy. That's the least of it."

"How so?" Darby smoothed hands across the long sleeves of her maroon crewneck shirt and absorbed the heat from the fire.

"My family and I...we were always at odds." He shared before draining the rest of his drink. "I didn't behave in a manner befitting a man who'd be *Lord* of the DeBurgh lands one day." The firelight cast a harsh glint to his profile then. "I've done so much to right it all the best way I can. If it works to plan maybe I'll even manage to put down a few roots."

Darby followed suit and drained the rest of her brandy. "Is that so important- putting down roots?'

Kraven looked her way. "I think it's important to know how you got here- who put you here."

Darby grimaced her disagreement. "Some roots are best left undisturbed."

"You really believe that?"

"I've always been afraid that's what my father's family would say if I ever had the nerve to meet them." She shook her head as if trying to dismiss unwanted thoughts. "I admire you for being brave enough to want that connection."

Kraven pulled her close and inhaled the floral scent of her curls. "You know I'm always there to help with those fears." He murmured, smiling when he felt her head bob as she chuckled.

◆　　◆　　◆

Two mornings later, a teary eyed Moira Bradenton stood outside the manor house hugging both Nile and Darby. Colin Bradenton was at work loading the car that would carry the women to the airport. Moira wished the young women a safe trip and asked that they not be strangers though it was obvious that she felt they'd be gone for good. Nile pulled out of the embrace when she saw Taurus walking around the side of the house with Kraven.

Darby kissed Moira's cheek and then went to hug Taurus. Next, she clasped hands with Kraven.

"Thanks so much for coming to *check* on me."

"Anytime."

Darby laughed. "You may want to reconsider that offer. Scotland isn't exactly a hop, skip and jump from California."

Kraven chuckled and tugged on the hem of Darby's fuzzy lavender sweater. "You know me…" he sighed with a wink. "I'll do anything to get away from a spider." He kissed her temple when she laughed again.

Taurus and Nile spoke no words at first and simply hugged by the car. She was shivering and by now, Taurus knew it had nothing to do with the chill in the air.

"Come back to me, alright?" He asked without expecting an answer.

Nile pressed her face into his neck inhaling the crisp scent of his cologne before she kissed him. "Goodbye," she whispered and disappeared into the car.

Taurus clenched a fist to still himself from going after her. Darby walked up and smoothed a hand across his back. He nodded leaning down to kiss her cheek and closing the door when she settled into the car. He knocked on the hood then urging Colin to drive on.

Kraven moved close to clap Taurus' shoulder. They watched the road dust whirl in the vehicle's wake.

◆　　◆　　◆

"What was Mommy thinking sleeping past five a.m.?" Michaela cooed while lifting a fussy Quincee from the crib.

The cooing turned Quinn's agitated whining into a more contented sound. Her silver gray stare twinkled in realization of her mother's face. Mick checked for wetness and then prepared to give the baby her feeding.

"Mommy has the lady's breakfast all ready," Mick sang softly while angling Quinn into the proper feeding position.

Quincee latched on easily and Mick began a slow rock of the chair. Still, her thoughts raced in the midst of the serene moment with her child.

Mother and daughter were cooing again by the time Quest awoke and came into the nursery. If possible, Quincee's expression grew more gleeful when she looked into her father's face. Her cooing rose to a delighted shrieking when Quest kissed her tiny mouth and nose. After several moments of play, he lifted her from Mick's arms and replaced her in the crib.

"How long are you gonna do this to me Mick?" He asked while stepping around the back of the rocker. "This is killing me," he folded his hands across the back of the chair to prevent the rocking.

Mick stared down at her hands clasped tightly in her lap. After a moment, she reached back and grabbed Quest's wrist pulling him around the chair and tugging until he was kneeling before her.

"I love you so much," she blinked tears from her lashes and searched his gorgeous dark face.

Quest trapped her neck in his hand holding her still for a kiss which was as punishing as it was passionate. "I love you," he reciprocated amidst the languid thrusts of his tongue inside her mouth. "Everything I do is-"

"To protect me. I know." She finished, swallowing when his haunting stare darkened in the telltale fashion that signaled the darkening of his mood. "You're suffocating me with this." She forced herself to finish. "Maybe protection at all costs is necessary to keep order in your family but I can't live like that. My independence-control in my life is too much a part of who I am-too much a part of my soul to be changed."

Scooting to the edge of the rocker, Mick cupped his face. "You'll lose me if you won't see that and I'm scared to death that you won't until it's too late." Pressing a quick kiss to his forehead, she left the chair and ran from the nursery.

◆　　◆　　◆

Minyon Oswald's round caramel brown face harbored a sympathetic expression when she glanced at the two men she escorted to her boss's office. "He's not in the best mood," she warned them and flexed her hands out of sheer nervousness. "In fact, he's been downright scary since he got back from that trip."

Moses grimaced and slanted a glance at Fernando. "Least we won't feel guilty about ruining his day with our news."

"Will you guys be needing anything?" Minyon asked when they stood outside the door to Taurus' office.

"How about holding his calls and no visitors for at least an hour after we leave?" Fernando asked, rubbing Minyon's arm when she nodded without hesitation.

Moses gave a quick knock upon the door.

"What?!"

The bellowing, unwelcoming salutation had the brothers inhaling deep breaths. Moses opened the door and he and Fernando bellowed their own words of greeting.

"Hell kid, you don't look like a man who's had close to a month's vacation!" Moses noted, ruffling his cousin's hair when he strolled behind the desk.

Taurus sat slumped in his chair and didn't bother to move his hand from over his eyes.

Moses perched on the edge of the desk. "Dena told us how much you liked Nile Becquois' show."

"Yeah, over two hundred K *much*," Fernando chipped in.

Taurus couldn't appreciate the teasing. "Right, and now I find out she's coming here to grace us with her presence." He tossed a glossy pamphlet across his desk. "An event at Charm Galleries," he explained and reclined in the desk chair. "Mel had 'em sent over this morning for us to put down in the lobby."

Moses scanned the colorful piece of literature. "At least that answers one question." He said and passed the pamphlet to Fernando.

"What?" Taurus asked having looked up in time to see the meaningful look pass between his cousins.

"We got news on Muhammad." Moses announced.

Taurus sat straight. "Go on."

"The daughter." Moses picked up the pamphlet. "Looks like she was under our noses the whole time. Nile Becquois."

Taurus looked from the pamphlet to Moses and began to shake his head. "No," he breathed standing from the chair.

"Seems so," Moses went on, tossing the pamphlet back to the desk. "She grew up in France with her mother until the woman died. She lived with her grandmother for a while. She was about seven when she went to live with Muhammad a short time after."

Taurus unbuttoned the hunter green suit coat and tugged at his tie but that did nothing to help his staggered breathing. He moved to sit on the edge of his desk, but missed. Fernando caught him seconds before he hit the floor.

Moses moved close and pressed his hands to Taurus's shoulders. "You gonna be alright?"

Taurus nodded but it was clear that he was anything but *alright*. "Can't be, can't be," he chanted.

"Everything checks out. She left for California when she was eighteen." Moses went on with his report. "The fact that she's doing this event with Ramsey could mean she's not connected with her father that way."

"Hell she may not even have those damn keys," Fernando mused folding his arms across his broad chest. "And if she does have them, she may be willing to cooperate just like we'd hoped."

Taurus waved his hand to silently signal that he wanted space. Moses and Fernando abided watching their cousin brace both hands on his desk and inhale huge amounts of air.

All the pieces were falling into place-all the things she'd said...hadn't said. Rage thickened inside Taurus like a noxious brew.

"I need to go," he decided suddenly.

"T," Moses called glancing toward Fernando for assistance when it was clear their cousin was hell bent on leaving the office.

"Easy man," Fernando urged, keeping his hold tight around Taurus' waist.

Moses cupped his face. "There's more T and it's best you hear it now."

◆    ◆    ◆

Darby relaxed on the sofa-the only furnishing in Nile's private studio at the condo she kept in L.A. "Are you sure about this?" She asked watching as her friend idly arranged tiny jars of paint.

"It's an excellent cause…" Nile shared, her tone was absent.

"And a *cause* Taurus could very well attend."

Nile nodded. "I thought of that."

"And?"

"I want to see him."

"Nile? Why? Why now?"

"I know it's crazy," Nile groaned leaving the shelf of paints to stand in the middle of the studio. "I want to see him just one last time. I want…to tell him everything." She nodded as though settling the idea in her mind. "He deserves to hear it from me."

"You do realize he probably already knows by now?"

Nile shook her head. "He doesn't know this."

The piercing green of Darby's gaze clouded with stunned surprise. "You're going to tell him that?"

"He deserves to know. He deserves to know why-why it can't work with us." Nile bowed her head. "Why I'm not the one he deserves."

Darby left the sofa and took Nile's arms in a firm grip. "You're exactly what he deserves-what he wants and needs."

"I only want to explain why. I can't expect him to look at me the same after this." Nile flinched a bit against Darby's hold. "I can't expect him to understand why I didn't tell him as soon as I found out who he was-who his sister was."

"Honey how could you possibly be so sure of how he'd react to this?"

"I knew what my father was doing. I was a child but I knew it was wrong. I tried so many times to get someone to pay attention to what I was trying to tell them…no one wanted to hear it. They were probably all involved. When I-when they sent me here I….let myself forget the horror of it. I just wanted to live new my life and pretend the other never happened."

Darby gave Nile a harsh shake. "Don't do that. Don't you dare stand there and blame yourself for that madness."

Nile didn't hear her. "In a round about way I asked him what he thought of Cufi Muhammad's daughter. He told me point blank what he thought…I don't expect any happy endings here D."

"So you can live with just walking away from him?" Darby marveled and stepped back to observe her friend.

Nile responded with a helpless shrug. "I already walked away from him but I took the truth with me and he needs that-he needs to have at least that. I can't give him much else but I can give him the full story and yeah D, I guess that I can live with."

# CHAPTER FOURTEEN

Charm Galleries swarmed with guests, paparazzi and beauty that evening. All of Seattle it seemed was on hand for the rare showing by the reclusive Nile Becquois. The artist actually rivaled her own work for beauty and mystique.

Nile arrived with Darby, Melina and Yohan. Shortly after, she was pulled in various directions for questions, photo-ops and autographs. Of course, Nile kept her mind on the cause and wasted no opportunity to speak on the evening's event. Proceeds would go to the Children's Art Board which would benefit urban youth in the Pacific Northwest. Those benefits would include funds for art supplies, classes and field trips. As a bonus, Nile's kids would also be obtaining a generous sum for their own artistic endeavors.

Nile was in the midst of answering questions about one of her racier pieces. The group surrounding her, included Quay, Fernando, Tykira and Contessa.

"So do you ever have problems with privacy?" Quay asked nodding toward the piece in question. "I guess tryin' to create this stuff would really draw a lot of attention-of the peeping tom variety."

"Nile forgive my husband," Ty urged once the laughter settled. "He loves your accent and just wants you to keep talking."

More laughter followed and Nile discovered that she was really enjoying herself. That is, until Taurus arrived with his sister on his arm. Her heart began a slow decent to her stomach and she willed herself to calm. Luckily, there was another question from a member of the press to draw her focus back to the business at hand.

Taurus was across the room and had already caught sight of Nile. Silently, he cursed her and then himself for not listening when she begged him to let her alone. Then, his expression grew impossibly harsh and he wondered if that was all a part of the plan. He walked off without a word to anyone.

Dena noticed. Her watchful eye followed her brother's movements as he crossed the gallery floor.

The auction portion of the event netted over $275K. Once Nile gave her final comments of the evening she left the stage to Melina and disappeared into the maze of first floor offices. She needed a minute to compose herself but almost reconsidered when she thought she heard a sound off one of the corridors. She decided against calling out shaking off thoughts that it could have been Taurus.

Several deep breaths were in order as she prepared to go out and face the music. She had to tell him then and there before she lost what little courage dwelled inside her. Giving one last tug to the white satin cuffs of her chic black cashmere frock, Nile gathered her belongings and re-entered the main gallery.

"Would you like us to bring a car around Ms. Becquois?" One of the hosts asked having noticed her wrap and purse.

"No need for that." Taurus spoke before Nile could say a word.

He kept her close, his hand smothering her upper arm in its grasp. Nile realized too late that she'd taken the hold as a sign of tenderness.

"I need to talk to you," she managed and felt the ice almost dripping from his words when he told her to 'save it'. Clearly he knew her connection to Cufi Muhammad. She was more thankful for the closeness then as it was the only thing keeping her on her feet.

As several photographers remained camped by the gallery entrance, Taurus took a less traveled route. In moments, they were leaving by a private exit.

"Thanks Rory," Taurus tipped the gentleman who'd been waiting near the mammoth Yukon Denali. "Get in," he told Nile the chill back in place as he held open the door to the navy blue SUV.

Nile obeyed and winced when the door slammed harshly at her ear. The ride began and was eerily silent as Taurus didn't see fit to even turn on the radio.

"Taurus-"

"I believe I asked you to 'save it'."

"Then why am I here?"

"Because I have things to say to you."

*And clearly they aren't nice things,* Nile acknowledged taking in the rigid set of his powerful lean form beneath the dark three piece suit he wore. Resting back against the seat, she decided to wait for whatever he threw at her. She tried to focus on anything other than the man she loved sitting next to her with ribbons of hate waving about him like a banner.

♦　　♦　　♦

Taurus parked the SUV and; with less ceremony than he'd used at the gallery, took Nile from the passenger side. She was so preoccupied by his mood that she had no time to register they were at her hotel until Taurus stopped right at her suite. Silently, he stood waiting for her to grasp that she was to open the door. Things finally clicked and she swiped the key card hurrying inside before he could take her arm in another vice hold.

Taurus closed the door softly and leaned against it with his arms folded. Nile knew the time for sweetness had long passed but that didn't stop her from watching him with clear love and longing in her eyes.

"So how far back did it go? When did you and daddy plan it?"

"Plan?" Nile barely whispered. All the things she'd wanted to tell him settled to the back of her throat as she waited.

Taurus pushed off the door and approached her on swift steps. "Understand that I'm not here to play twenty questions. My temper is not something you want directed at you." He cupped her chin but it wasn't meant to be an act of tenderness. "It would be unwise for you to act like you have no idea what I'm asking you."

The warning was clear. Nile realized nothing she'd imagined came close to how viciously the hate would actually appear in his crystalline stare. Focusing then on his questions and less on her nerves, she clutched her hands and summoned her voice.

"I don't associate with my father. I've lived in this country since I was eighteen and I've been successful at avoiding any meetings with him regardless of how hard he's tried. I'd allowed myself to believe my mother when she told me they were going to shut it all down-that it was over. But I had no contact with my father. I never visited or saw him until several months ago," she spoke up suddenly when his expression grew fiercer. "He-he came to see me at the place I keep in Hawaii. It was a fluke that he found me there-he showed up completely out of the blue…I realized why he was there when I heard about…Zara." She turned away from Taurus and stared out across the living area as though she were envisioning the meeting. "He was there talking to me like a proud father. I-I told him I never wanted anyone to know I had his blood. He left eventually and it wasn't until after that visit that I thought of the box of cards. That's what he came for."

"So you do have them?"

Nile whirled around and nodded. "My mother sent them two-three years ago. She told me things were getting weird. She didn't say how only that she wasn't sure what my father's plans for them were. She said…they were her tickets and-and mine. She told me they'd protect me-my life." She focused on her fingertips grown red from how tightly she'd clenched them. "I didn't know what they were for exactly but I recognized some of the faces-*vaguely*…I was sure they were men I'd seen…I never helped devise any scheme Taurus," she swore praying for a sign that his demeanor was softening. There was none. "I let myself forget where I came from, what I am…what my parents were doing. I can't stand to be in the same room with them let alone help them to defend their sick lifestyle."

"Yet you kept the cards anyway."

"I was afraid! I-I knew those were powerful people. The things I'd seen… I didn't know if I'd be putting my kids in danger and then-then there was you and your family." She shook her head and moved closer to him. "I was going to give them to you."

"When? In Scotland? When you told me you loved me? When Nile?"

"I came here to give them to you."

"Thought you came here to sell paintings?"

"After-"

"Is that right?" He interjected, questioning her in the style that made him so successful in the courtroom. "Let's have 'em then."

Nile smoothed both hands down the sides of her dress and cursed her decision to let Darby keep the keys in her room. She hadn't wanted them any closer than necessary until it was time to turn them over.

"Well?" Taurus prompted, looking as though he knew she couldn't produce the goods.

"I don't have them here I-"

"But you came here to give them up, right?"

"Yes, but-"

"That's what you said, right?"

"Please. Please Taurus you have to believe-"

Taurus muttered an oath that stopped her words and then he was taking her arm in another hold that sparked shards of pain.

"You know what I believe?" He murmured close to her face, his light eyes narrowed with murderous intent. "I believe that shit between us was all to…encourage me and my family to back off."

Nile began to shake her head.

"I fall for you and when I finally learn that the love of my life is Cufi Muhammad's baby girl, I'd just be too crazy in love to take down her dear daddy."

Nile was shaking her head more feverishly and trying to ignore the pain that mercifully dimmed thanks to the numbness overtaking her arm.

Taurus was struggling to ignore pain as well. It shredded his heart with such vengeance he could scarcely breathe.

"Please…" she begged through the tears and emotion constricting her throat.

Taurus stifled whatever sympathy threatened to break through his rage. His free hand closed around her throat. "You know this plan would've probably worked if you'd told me everything in Scotland while I was stupid for you and actually thinking you were the woman I'd give my life for."

"Taurus," she curled her hands over his wrist.

He ignored her. "Maybe if you'd told me then, I would've done anything-believed anything you said."

Nile could plead no more. The tears took over and she stood there before him crying like a child. Taurus knew he was on the verge of tears as well but again he set aside sympathetic urges and replaced them with rage.

"I gotta hand it to Cufi, he spared no expense." He let go of her neck. "Saved his best little whore to come and try to get the job done."

Nile blinked. As if he'd hit her, all the pain and upset was flushed away by shock. She barely registered dropping to the sofa when he released her.

The tirade and her reaction to it seemed to zap Taurus' anger then. He knew there was nothing to be said that would undo the damage he'd done to her. Forcing himself to back away, he headed for the door and left her alone.

The shock gradually wore off, but the numbness remained. Nile was just pulling herself from the sofa when a knock sounded on the suite door. She watched it knowing she could take no more accusations that night. Still; knowing Taurus could be there and that she could have another chance at making him understand, overruled. Dismissing her unease, she rushed to the door and wrenched it open with his name on her lips. Instead of Taurus, she found three men filling the doorway. They gave her no choice but to back away and let them enter.

"Congratulations on a very fine show Mademoiselle Becquois," the shorter slender man commended.

"What do you want?" Nile asked, not liking the grins and leering gazes of the two giants who stood behind the talker.

The slender man glanced back and up at his associates as well. "What *they* want will be very taxing on your lovely body unless you give me what *I* want."

Nile took a step back. Her guests followed.

"Think think Ms. Becquois. You give me what I want and we leave." He shrugged. "You keep acting like you know nothing about those card keys and

I go back and report to my boss while leaving you with my boys here. And let me assure you, they have very…extensive appetites."

Nile needed no further explanations. "They're here-secured in town. I can take you to them." She bartered; her intention was to get out of the suite and down to the crowded lobby.

Frank Deeks smiled, knowing his very real threat would do the trick. Brogue Tesano would be pleased as he frowned on the physical abuse of women. Frank waved a hand toward Nile. "After you, Mademoiselle."

As Nile hoped, the lobby was packed. Whatever plans she had to call for help once the elevator doors opened, fizzled when she felt the barrel of a gun at her spine.

"No sudden moves now." Frank Deeks warned.

Nile was scrambling to coordinate another plan when she saw someone familiar heading towards her. She and her three escorts had no choice but to stop when Dena Ramsey stood before them.

"Dena what-what are you doing here?" Nile's eyes relayed the panic she was desperate to keep from her voice.

"I know Taurus is raging. My brother's temper can make him say and do awful things Nile. None of this is your fault and I didn't want him coming down on you for it."

Nile shuddered. "He's already come and gone Dena." She shared, bristling when one of her escorts pressed the gun deeper into her spine.

"Damn," Dena grumbled and dragged a hand through her wavy dark hair. "I'm so sorry girl. I tried to get here before, but that gallery was so crazy and it took a while before I even realized you were gone."

"It's okay Dena really. Why don't you go on back and I'll call you before I leave."

"That won't be necessary. Ms. Ramsey's welcomed to walk out with us as well." Frank Deeks invited, smiling at the quick glance Dena flashed his way.

"I uh, don't want to keep you," Dena was saying while every part of her shrieked that something was very wrong.

Frank stepped closer. "I'm afraid I'm gonna have to insist." He said and pulled back his lapel so that she could see his gun.

Dena smothered her scream, grabbed Nile's hand and turned to do as instructed. When they were outside, Frank leaned over and inserted his head between Nile's and Dena's.

"My boss likes to keep things neat," he said, "but he's assured me that I should take any precautions to ensure cooperation. Ms. Becquois can fill you in on what I mean Ms. Ramsey."

Nile squeezed Dena's hand reassuringly though her confidence was quickly dwindling. They crossed over into the outdoor parking deck which was void of the heavy traffic on hand in the lobby.

"Now where are they?" Frank demanded grabbing Nile suddenly and hauling her against the back of an SUV.

Dena screamed and one of the giants jerked her back by the collar of her blouse. When she struggled, he issued a silent warning by setting his gun in place against her neck.

Nile's thoughts were as disjointed as a thousand loose puzzle pieces. She was struggling to come up with a lie to pacify the men when she caught sight of movement behind the giant holding Dena. Before she could lock in on the figure, Dena screamed again as she was thrown clear of her captor.

Frank Deeks whirled around with Nile plastered against his chest. Horrified, he watched one of his associates have his neck broken while the other suffered a chop to the throat which killed him instantly. Frank shoved Nile against Carlos McPherson and ran before he too lost his life at the hands of the effective killer.

Both women were shaky but alive. Carlos was satisfied and decided not to give chase. He kept Nile close and opened an arm to Dena who buried her face in his chest as she whispered his name.

"How did you know?" Dena asked, looking way up into his gorgeous honey-toned face.

Carlos kissed Dena's temple and closed his eyes to offer a prayer of gratitude. "Your cousin asked me to keep an eye on you-something I was already doing."

Dena could only shudder and turned her face back into his chest.

Nile was still on edge but smiled at the love radiating between the two people next to her. As grateful as she was for her life, a part of her died over the love she'd lost that night.

# *CHAPTER FIFTEEN*

Taurus had thundered out of the Sorenson Hotel and into his Denali with plans to head back to the gallery and enjoy the evening and forget Nile Becquois ever existed. He'd accomplished the thundering out and *heading* out, but going back to the gallery and enjoying the evening were hollow intentions.

As for forgetting Nile Becquois ever existed, he had a better chance of forgetting to breathe.

"Idiot!" He whispered viciously to himself and rubbed the back of his hand against the corner of his eye. Surprise registered on his face when he saw moisture clinging to his skin.

*The things he said to her...*No one deserved that, least of all her. She'd been sired by a monster but blood was the only thing she shared with Cufi Muhammad. She was good and Taurus knew that the first time he met her. The beauty she seemed so wary of was only an enchanting case for the true beauty that resided at the heart of her.

He stopped the Denali suddenly amidst screeching tires along with flagrant horn blowing and curses from angry drivers. He whipped the massive vehicle back in the direction he'd come. His mind raced with thoughts of what to say to her. What words could he speak that could ever make up for the cruelty he'd unfairly spouted before. He'd say-do whatever he had to. He'd do whatever she asked.

*And if she asks you to get the hell out of her sight?* His heart jerked at the possibility. Of course he knew she'd have every right to demand it and he'd have no choice but to obey.

◆　　◆　　◆

Nile and Dena sat in silence for at least fifteen minutes once Carlos had taken them out to Yohan and Melina's. The ordeal they'd shared earlier that night was long passed yet the memories of what could've been, replayed vividly and often.

"Carlos is incredible," Nile spoke in a tone of awe.

Dena smirked. "Always has been."

Nile squeezed her hands around the mug of hot tea she held. "I saw a lot of love there. I'm thinking it wasn't just because of tonight."

Dena shook her head. "I've loved Carlos McPherson since his family moved to Seattle when we were all in high school."

"But you never got together?"

"Things happened."

Nile bowed her head and set aside her mug.

"Until a few weeks ago, I'd forgotten that day in the spa." Dena said

Nile's head snapped up and she found the woman looking right at her.

"I remembered the way you looked at my scar. You were in a one-piece but I got the feeling you recognized it." Dena's eyes drifted downward. "I also got the feeling that maybe you have one just like it."

"I'm so sorry," Nile gasped, barely able to see Dena beyond the tears pooling her dark eyes. "So horrific," She continued swallowing past the dread lodged in her throat. "My father-what they did was so horrific and I just…I just let myself forget. I didn't want to remember it. I'm so very sorry."

Dena clutched Nile's hand. "You have nothing to be sorry for-nothing. Do you hear me?"

"But what my father did-"

"Was *not* your fault. I was there because of my father too, remember?"

They met in a hug across the arms of their chairs. Time ticked on for more than a few minutes before Nile spoke.

"Your brother hates me now. He'll loathe me when he hears this."

"My brother loves you."

Nile shook her head against Dena's shoulder. "No-no I expected him to be angry that I hid who my father was but he actually believes the things I said to him-did…with him were all a part of some plan."

"I don't care what he said. *I don't care.*" Dena emphasized and pulled back to look at Nile's face. "Taurus can barely think straight he loves you so. All this has got his mind so turned around…once he comes down off it, he'll find you with his hat and his guilt in hand."

Nile couldn't argue further and simply held Dena's hand. They were in silence when a knock rapped on the den door. It was Carlos. Dena went right to him where they hugged for the longest time.

"Are you okay?" Carlos was asking Nile as he looked over the top of Dena's head.

Nile's smile was shaky but it was there. "I'm fine. Thank you so much Carlos."

He nodded and then looked down and pinched Dena's chin. "Does the fact that I saved your life tonight grant me time to talk to you?"

"Grants you as much time as you want." Dena said, unabashed tears radiating from her gaze.

"Forever?" Carlos inquired.

Dena stood on her toes and hugged him tighter. "That's a good start." She whispered.

◆　◆　◆

The fear that gripped Taurus since he stepped foot back inside the Sorenson, gave way to sheer terror when he was questioned by an officer before being granted access to Nile's room floor. Once off the elevator, his identification was confirmed a second time. Taurus ordered himself not to run to Nile's room once he was given permission to proceed. He didn't know whether to feel relieved or become completely unhinged at the sight of Moses in the corridor just outside her room.

"Where is she?" Taurus clutched the front of his cousin's suit coat and backed the man against a wall.

"She's fine." Moses' assurance was soft and he didn't try to undo the death grip Taurus had on his clothes. "She's at Yohan and Melina's with Dena."

"Dena?" Taurus whispered as his frown took on a fiercer element. "What happened?" He listened as Moses gave a condensed but terrifyingly accurate account of the evening's events. After hearing the tale, he made a move for the elevators when he caught sight of Darby in the living area of her room.

"Hey?" He knocked once against the doorjamb. "You okay?" He asked, stepping past the open door.

Darby nodded though it was obvious she'd been crying heavily. "I can't believe they just came in here and grabbed her like that…" The brave front she'd tried to keep in place, dissolved as her tears resumed.

"Hey, hey, shh…" Taurus pulled her into a rocking embrace.

"And your sister they-they just took them…" Darby shuddered against Taurus' shoulder. "God Taurus what kind of people are these?"

"Listen to me, Nile and my sister are alright. You hear me? I want you to calm down okay?" He gave the order in the quiet, rough tone of his voice that had her nodding as if mesmerized. "I'm on my way to see Nile. Do you need anything before I go?"

Darby shook her head. "Your cousin Moses and his men are taking care of it. They arranged for us to move to the penthouse suite at the Montgomery until it's time to leave."

Taurus nodded and pressed a kiss to the curls shielding her forehead. "I'll leave you to it then," he decided.

"Taurus wait," Darby called, "there's something..." her voice trailed away as she moved deeper into the suite. She returned to the front holding what looked to be a locked box. She handed it over and smiled when he watched her blankly. "She said they were card keys. She gave them to me for safe keeping but she wanted you to have them. Is this what they came after her for?"

Taurus was too devastated to offer a response. Weakened by a new wave of guilt, he lost his hold on the box and it crashed to the floor. "Make sure Moses gets them," he managed to instruct as a round of nausea rumbled through his stomach. Closing his eyes briefly, he struggled to get his bearings and then rushed from the room.

◆　　◆　　◆

"Alright well I guess that's everything. The kitchen is at the end of the hall but you just yell for me or Yohan if you need anything, okay?" Melina was saying as she helped Nile settle in. Mel's slanting stare was filled with uncertainty as she gazed upon the cozily made pullout sofa bed. "Girl, are you sure about sleeping down here in the den? We've got tons of guestrooms."

Nile smoothed her hands along the sleeves of her black and white striped cotton robe. She smiled at the dim casual elegance of the room that had already cast a strangely comforting sensation upon her. "I appreciate it Melina, but I really don't want to be anywhere else."

Mel shrugged. "Well only if you're sure..."

"I am-honest," Nile sighed even as unease reclaimed its place in her eyes. "You're very kind and I...I know it's difficult having me here."

Mel dimmed the lights and decided to let the blaze from the fireplace illuminate the den. "What do you mean-difficult?"

Nile moved closer to the fireplace as well. "Taurus told me about your cousin-Zara. I know my father was responsible for what happened to her and-"

"That's right Nile. Your *father*-your father was responsible."

"But I-"

"Had nothing to do with it," Mel said, her tilted stare focused and firm. "Listen to me Nile. If I'm gonna stand here and condemn you because of who your father is well hell I'd have to disown my husband and much of his family."

Nile surprised herself when a bellow of laughter forced its way out of her chest.

"No more of this, alright?" Mel ordered extending her hand.

Powerfully moved, Nile could only nod and stepped in to relish the hug Mel gave.

Melina left Nile relaxing in the den. She turned down the electric candles lighting the lower level and was on her way upstairs when the knocker dropped against the front door. Changing directions, she checked the looking window and saw Taurus outside. She opened the door and pointed left. "In the den," she instructed.

Taurus kissed Mel's cheek and set out. His steps were surprisingly firm until he rounded the corner and approached the door. There, he only stood unable to move a step further.

Nile opted for a cup of tea before turning in. She was shrugging back into her robe while pulling open the den door. Finding Taurus in the hall shut down everything inside her. Speaking was impossible, breathing a chore. She retreated as he advanced and closed the door. For a time they watched one another. Nile backed away a little every few seconds-anticipating more harsh words. Nothing prepared her for the three he uttered.

"Forgive me please."

She stilled, certain she'd mistaken him.

"I don't know what right I have to stand here and dare hope you could after the way I treated you," he said shaking his head and sounding as if he were speaking to himself. "What I said…damaged you," he continued, shoving his hands into the pockets of the dark trousers he wore. His shirt hung wrinkled outside his pants and accentuated his haggard appearance. "You didn't deserve that," he acknowledged and smirked in disgust at his actions. "Of all the people I know, you're the very last who deserved that."

"It's alright Taurus-"

"No it's not," he argued frowning a bit at how easily she accepted the ugliness. "The time's come for you to stop wearing the guilt for your father. I took you right back to that with the things I said and I *am* sorry. I can never make up for it, but I pray you can forgive me."

Nile's lashes fluttered and she wanted to run to him. She wanted to lose herself in his embrace-in the love she saw in his eyes again. Unfortunately, there was more to be said-more he needed to know.

"When my father started his…brothel he had plans-plans for it to be much more than a place where men came to indulge fantasies. I didn't understand that then, but being away from him, growing up and coming to…learn what it was all about I eventually got it. He wanted to have a place where some could make fortunes with him to thank."

"Honey you don't have to tell me this." Taurus soothed. His features were softened by sympathy.

"I need to finish this." She argued, her dark eyes narrowed with certainty. "The girls that he…victimized were valuable for more than the money they made on their backs. Two of his *clients* had connections to certain *markets* that provided exceedingly wealthy people with items that were more valuable than money." She shivered as buried memories resurfaced. "They were markets that provided wealthy couples who couldn't have children with the means to have them."

Taurus felt the nausea returning and knew the rest of Nile's story would require him to sit.

"But for certain women it's about more than having the baby." Nile continued once Taurus sat perched on the back of the sofa. "They wanted the experience and that meant conceiving and it's difficult to conceive when there are problems with ones ovaries."

Slowly, Taurus' stunning gaze raked the length of Nile's body. "What are you telling me?"

Nile pressed her lips together and worried the belt around her robe. Silently, she begged her tears to wait. "These women…rich women couldn't conceive because of … '*Infertility due to rapid loss of ovarian follicles*'. She gave the more scientific explanation. "So there became an interest in donation-*ovarian* donation." Nervously, she tugged on a lock of her hair. "There are many women who make good money doing this willingly. But why go looking for someone you'd have to pay or counsel when you've got the producers on staff." She tilted back her head to prevent a tear from escaping her eye. "Those girls made money using their bodies in more ways than one."

Taurus closed his eyes while dragging fingers through his hair.

Nile turned, her lovely dark face void of emotion. "This was no *donation*. It was a harvesting to acquire ovarian tissue to be cultivated for fertilization or in some cases they were used to create an embryo, transplant it, cause a pregnancy…"

"Jesus…" Taurus breathed.

"The men at the head of the whole thing…they had to be sure that other potential investors could be controlled. They had to be sure that the organization was protected should these investors ever have a crisis of conscience or threaten blackmail. For my father this opportunity was too delicious to pass up. After all, he had prime ovary donors right at his disposal-their bodies were his."

Taurus was riveted on the story and dared not move from his place on the sofa.

"He'd make a fine addition to their business once he met certain requirements."

"Which were?"

"In spite of the obscene amounts of front money these investors were asked to produce, there was more. The *powers that be* wanted the investors to have as much to lose by joining as they did by letting them in."

"What did he do to you?" Taurus whispered, the quiet roughness of his voice laced with an unmistakably deadly undertone.

Nile went on feeling progressively lighter as she purged the story. "There were many ways to encourage loyalty. But the men with daughters were required to present them for a simple procedure to…remove what was more valuable than money."

"Son of a bitch!" Taurus pressed a clenched fist to his mouth to tamp down his anger.

Nile's heart was in her throat as she remembered it. "I was almost fifteen. Something-something went wrong during…I can never have children. My father acted like I'd just had my tonsils removed. No feeling…no remorse. At that time there was no proof that this would even work." She laughed at the cold and utter uselessness of it all. "It was just a simple experiment you see? Nothing to fret over." She restated the explanations her father had given. "He and your uncle were two of a kind." She whispered.

"Marcus."

Nile's expression was closed. "He was another investor." She confirmed and waited for him to realize.

It didn't take long and soon Taurus shook his head. "But Marc…he wouldn't have had a daughter to provide."

"No, but your father did."

"My father…Dena? No…" He shook his head frantically then as he watched Nile nod. "No…" he groaned then as his amber stare filled with disbelief.

"I knew in Montenegro when I saw her in the spa at the hotel-just before we left. I saw the scar-same as mine." She brushed her fingers across the spot where the lacy gray gown covered her belly. Her cheeks were already wet when she noticed the first tears finally spilling from her eyes. "My biggest fear now is what will happen to all those girls- those rescued girls and women. They know way too much for the people at the head of all this not to go after them."

"God," he murmured as if stunned. The tears flowed more freely. Unashamed, he gave in to them. He'd been prepared for the anger, but the hurt and grief took him completely off guard.

Nile ached to hold him, but not knowing how he'd accept her closeness, kept her at bay. When she would've moved back another step, he reached out and pulled her close. Taurus nuzzled his head into her belly and cried for his sister, his mother and the woman he loved.

Nile didn't try to silence him knowing he'd needed the release for weeks-possibly years. She threaded her fingers through his hair and waited.

◆　　◆　　◆

"So what was it like being from France and living in Compton?"

Nile laughed. It was much later and they sat camped around the island in Yohan and Melina's kitchen with a pot of berry coffee between them. "You know, no one's ever asked me that before." She sobered after a while. "My mom's family was wonderful and they never made me feel like an outsider. My Aunt Reesy was like the matriarch of the neighborhood or something-everyone wanted to please her so...I got the royal treatment."

Taurus' gaze grew softer. "I think they'd have given you that no matter whose niece you were." He predicted and laughter resounded again.

"I want you to forgive me Nile." He was saying once the silence had lengthened between them. "I need you to...but is it possible for you to do that while you're thinking about when you want to marry me?"

"Marry?" Nile gasped almost losing her grip on the mug she held in shaking hands. "After what I told you-what happened to Dena-"

"Wasn't your fault."

"Alright, alright I understand that. I do," she insisted when he watched her doubtfully. "I know I wasn't there with the scalpel but every time you look at me you'll think of what she went through, no?"

Taurus moved off the high-backed stool and stood over Nile. He cupped his hands around her neck and tipped back her chin with his thumbs.

"When I look at you I see the woman I love. I see the woman I think of when I wake. And when I fall asleep at night you're the woman I dream of. I can't see anyone else but you-I'm ruined here."

"So am I." Nile countered, though her meaning was far different. "I can't give you children-the thing you want most."

"Sperm doesn't make a father nor do ovaries or the lack thereof make a mother." He argued. "What I want most is you for my wife-nothing more-nothing less."

"Taurus," she whispered as his lips touched hers.

The kiss lasted for a sweet moment. Then Taurus lifted her from the island and carried her back into the den. He kept her beneath him on the sofa bed where he became absorbed by her. He was like a man possessed and starved, kissing and suckling madly down the length of her body as he tugged away her gown. He paid special attention to the dreaded scar and kissed it with a passion that stilled Nile's breath. His luxurious hair caressed her skin with its silken feel as he made his way downward. He feasted upon the heart of her, nibbling the extra sensitive bud of desire that had her trembling into the bed coverings. Tirelessly, he drank in her essence until she cried out for something more satisfying than his tongue.

His patience at an end, Taurus wasted no time in obliging her request. When he was inside her, he simply rested his head on her shoulder and relished the way she gloved him. Nile bit her lip to keep from screaming her approval when he moved slowly thrusting, rotating, branding her with his desire and love.

Afterwards, they remained locked in a lover's embrace. They were thoroughly spent, thoroughly in love and thoroughly optimistic of their future.

# CHAPTER SIXTEEN

Moses was reviewing his decisions regarding protection for the family. Of course, special emphasis on protection referred to Dena and Nile.

"We need to act fast where these keys are concerned." Moses told his brother and cousin.

"Where is my sister exactly?" Taurus asked while topping off his coffee.

"Carlos has her-didn't say where he was goin' with her just that she was his." Moses announced with a smirk.

Fernando chuckled. "Damn right."

Taurus raised his mug in a mock toast. "Damn time." He agreed.

"And what about Nile?" Moses asked Taurus. "You okay with her out at Yohan and Mel's?"

Taurus nodded. "For now. Besides, she's comfortable there and Yohan keeps that place more secure than Fort Knox."

"I still plan to have more of my men add to that security."

"You think them fools will come after her again?" Fernando asked.

"In a heartbeat." Taurus figured. "And I suspect Cufi will be getting in touch as well."

Moses nodded. "You think he'd risk it?"

"He wants those keys. He and Yvonne."

Moses glanced at Fernando. "You think we can grab 'em both?"

Taurus shrugged. "Maybe it'll help not to have your men hovering too close." He suggested and finished up his coffee. "We done?" he asked.

"Not quite." Moses said while leaning over his desk. "Just one more thing to take care of. I'd say we've waited long enough."

"So he's coming in today?" Taurus asked, knowing what Moses was referring to. Reclaiming his seat, he waited in heavy silence with his cousins until the office door opened and Quest walked inside.

"So serious," Quest noted, closing the distance to shake hands and hug his family. "How are Dena and Nile?" he asked Taurus.

"Good. Carlos has Dena with him and Nile's out at Yohan and Mel's. Moses is gonna add more men out there to keep an eye on things. We've decided to set a meeting next week to discuss the keys."

Quest nodded while rubbing his hands together. "Sounds like everything's in place-exactly why'd you guys need to see me?"

Moses waved toward an empty chair and waited for his cousin to sit. "Ever heard of a man named Charlton Browning?"

"Should I have?" Quest asked.

Moses came round to sit on the edge of his desk. "Browning witnessed a murder and was a protected witness, but the *authorities* protecting him were more interested in protecting information he had on them-interests in young girls."

Quest shifted in his seat. His expression sharpened slightly but he said nothing.

"They helped him disappear." Moses continued. "They helped set him up in style in his chosen profession-helped him change his name to Cufi Muhammad." Moses let the information settle while focusing on the toe of his navy boots before he went on. "A few weeks ago Mick came to see me asking for my help in finding out whatever I could."

Hearing Michaela's name, Quest's expression darkened as his gaze narrowed toward Moses. "Why is my wife looking for Cufi Muhammad?"

"She's not. She's looking for Charlton Browning-the man who dated her mother. The man who took her mother away from her."

"No."

"Yvonne Wilson was born Evette Sellars. She left Compton California for Chicago where she changed her name just before leaving with Muhammad-leaving her eight year old daughter behind."

"Who else knows about this?" Quest managed to ask, though his chest felt as though it was about to explode.

"I had to tell County," Fernando shared raising his hand when Quest glared his way. "Don't worry. She's too upset to say a thing."

"And Nile?" Quest was focused on Taurus then.

"I haven't told her, but Q I've seen photos of Yvonne Wilson and Mick is almost the splitting image of her. Won't take long for Nile to make the connection," he said and recognized the devastation blooming in his cousin's eyes. "Listen, we understand if you want us to wait until you tell Mick-"

"I'm not telling Mick."

"We understand man," Fernando was saying. "It's a lot to swallow and we know it'll take time for you to get around to-"

"I'm not ever telling her." Quest said and watched his cousins exchange looks.

"That's a mistake Q," Taurus warned. "I just found out first hand how much worse things can get if they're kept in the dark too long."

"I'm not ever telling her. That's all." Quest said once more, the firmness in his now black stare warned everyone to let go of the argument.

Moses stood before Quest then. "T's right man-it's a mistake to keep this. This is Mick we're dealing with, you know?"

Smiling in a half-amused, half-dangerous manner, Quest stepped close to his cousin. "You're telling me how to handle my wife now, Mo?"

Moses treaded carefully. Having often been accused of being the most unsettling Ramsey, he recognized the look of a more challenging opponent. While his *looks* gave him the aura of unsettling, Moses knew that the unsettling persona went all the way to Quest's soul.

"Q, she's already come to me for information on the man," Moses warned gently. "She'll get suspicious if I take too long to give her something. Not to mention Yvonne Wilson. If Nile can see a resemblance, what do you think Mick's gonna do if she sees her?"

"You should listen to Moses, Q," Taurus chimed softly. "Better for her to hear this now from you, than in some other messed up way."

"Are we done here?" Quest asked watching his cousins sigh as if they'd accepted the fact that they would not change his mind.

Moses raised his hands and Quest left without a backward glance. In the dim hall outside the office, he lost strength to stand and leaned against the wall-head bowed, eyes closed.

◆　　◆　　◆

A few evenings later, Nile ventured out with her bodyguards trailing. She headed to Charm Galleries hoping her pieces from the exhibit were still on display. Mel caught sight of Nile shortly after she'd arrived and scolded her for not saying anything about wanting to visit the gallery.

"We could've driven in together." Mel said once she and Nile hugged.

"I just decided to come and I wanted to get here late-miss all that traffic." Nile explained. "Taurus is going to meet me for dinner. I just needed to be around my stuff even if it's not *mine* anymore. It calms me still."

Melina rubbed her hand along the fuzzy gray cotton sleeve of Nile's dress. "I understand and you take all the time you need. I'm on my way home unless you want me to stay til T gets here?"

Nile shook her head. "There's no need, but thanks-the guards are here so…"

Mel's slanting stare narrowed a bit more. "I can't see anyone who looks like a guard."

Nile bumped shoulders with Melina. "That's the idea. They're supposed to be keeping a low profile."

"Ah….well I'll leave you to it then. There're a few last browsers but they shouldn't get in your way. Now you've got the house number, right?" Mel inquired with a raised brow.

Nile patted her purse. "Programmed in my cell."

"Good girl." Mel whispered and pulled Nile into another hug. "I'm gonna stop and ask my guards to keep an eye on you as well-low profile of course." She said with a wink.

Alone then, Nile hugged herself while strolling about the area that sheltered her work. Feeling instantly relaxed, she delighted in all that she had and all that she'd found. She heard her name and turned expecting to see Taurus. Finding Cufi Muhammad there instead, brought a noticeable chill to her expression.

"How'd you get in here?" She asked her father.

Cufi raised his hands slightly. "It's a gallery love-many perspective buyers," A tinge of regret darkened his brown eyes then. "I have many apologies to give, I guess."

"Save them." Nile spat in French. "They come too late and you have too many to give."

Cufi bowed his head to acknowledge the truth in that fact. "I understand that you never want to see me again. I'm prepared to abide by that."

"Once I give you the card keys?" Nile predicted watching as her father's face shone with realization.

"I suppose your mother told you what they were?"

"Doesn't matter now," Nile confirmed with a quick shake of her head.

Cufi slipped both hands in the pockets of his tan trousers. "If she told you what they were, surely she told you how valuable they are."

"And that's why you're here."

"They'll get me back on my feet."

"Right…back to selling little girls."

Cufi bristled. "You never have to be bothered by any of that. Ever. Just tell me where the keys are."

"In the hands of the Ramseys," Nile announced with relish shining on her oval face.

Whatever softness dwelled on Cufi's face vanished as if it had never existed. "What did you do?" He asked, a vicious curl beginning to tug at his lip.

Nile planted her feet squarely. "What should've been done a long time ago."

"You little idiot! You backstabbing little…to betray your own father-"

"A l'enfer avec vous!" *To hell with you*, she raged. "You stand there and talk to me about betrayal after the horror you put me and all those kids through?"

"The things I gave you… a lifestyle few could ever dream of."

"Mmm oui Papa. It boggles my mind when I think of all the things *afforded* in my lifestyle with you." Rolling her eyes, Nile turned her back. "Get out of my sight." She ordered.

Cufi stood there unable to move but for the intermitted clenching and unclenching of his fists. Then as though all the frustrations and gravity of the dire situation were welling inside him, he let out a pained sound and charged for his daughter.

Nile turned stunned and unprepared to react as the distance closed between them.

"Cufi!" Yvonne Wilson cried her husband's name seconds before the gun she carried fired six shots into his chest.

Somehow, Cufi remained standing his expression frozen in disbelief. Then, he crumpled to the gallery floor between his wife and daughter. Despite her anger towards him, Nile felt the loss shudder through her like a sickness.

Yvonne let her hands fall but held onto the gun. She raised a tearful gaze to Nile whose name she bellowed before anything more could be said.

Nile turned finding Taurus storming towards her. She ran to him without another glance at her parents.

"Drop the gun Ms. Wilson!" The guards ordered simultaneously and moved in much the same manner.

Yvonne obeyed without hesitation. Two guards took her by the arms and she was prepared to go willingly until she realized that they weren't leading her toward Nile but in the opposite direction.

"My daughter-"

"Sorry Ms. Wilson we can't allow that just yet." The on-scene detective explained.

"I saved her."

"That may be, but you have questions to answer."

The sound of sirens in the distance triggered Yvonne's panic and then she began to struggle heartily against the powerful holds on her arms.

"Nile!" She screamed as she was lead away. "Nile?! Nile!" her voice went hoarse as the cries intensified.

"Shh…" Taurus soothed squeezing his eyes shut tight and inhaling Nile's scent.

"How'd you know…something was wrong?" Her voice shuddered uncontrollably.

Taurus pressed a kiss to her temple and uttered a quiet prayer. "We'd been watching from a distance. We hoped he'd feel comfortable enough to approach you eventually. God…" He kissed her temple again. "I should've suspected he'd turn on you. Damn I should've known…"

As he held her shuddering form, Nile gathered what strength she had and built the nerve to ask him.

"How?" Her voice was muffled against his neck. She pulled back as far as he'd allow. "How could you want to be with me- be a part of me, when I come from…from this?" She looked back at her father's dead body. Wrenching away from Taurus then, she fixed him with a stern dark look. "Do you know what you're getting into?" Her voice was a whisper.

"Why would you ask me that?" Taurus' gaze narrowed as his temper stirred.

Nile looked back at Cufi. This time, Taurus took her chin in his hand and made her face him.

"Things change when a person has a chance to sleep on it," she said, her voice wavering on the fear that she was about to lose him. "You may feel differently in the morning."

Taurus hissed a sudden curse and pulled her tight against him. "Let me tell you this, and I don't expect to have to constantly repeat it," he smoothed the hand that held her chin around to cup her face. "For at least the next sixty years, the only thing I plan to sleep on is you."

"Taurus…"

"Believe me, believe me…" he chanted, pumping his hand around her cheek until she began to nod.

"Believe me," he said once more before he jerked her into a hug of promise and devotion.

Nile shuddered and cuddled closer to Taurus. She absorbed the life and love radiating from his body and into hers. She held onto him tighter still while drifting farther away from the death and hate that moved into her past.

# EPILOGUE

## *Near Invernesshire, Scotland~*

Beneath overcast yet breathtaking skies, Taurus Ramsey and Nile Becquois were married. They stood on their favorite hillside surrounded by love and the family and friends who adored them.

Taurus felt his wife shudder in his arms and looked down to find her cheeks wet. "I hope those are happy tears?" He teased.

"Nothing but happiness," she confirmed. "I thought I'd never see this place again. I never dreamed if I did we'd be getting married here."

"A lot to take in." Taurus acknowledged.

"A lot but never too much," Nile vowed turning in her husband's arms.

"Never?" he probed.

"Never."

Brushing the back of his hand across her cheek, Taurus leaned in. He and Nile shared the sweetest kiss and whispered 'I love you' in unison.

♦   ♦   ♦

## *Savannah, Georgia~*

"Good work. Exceptional. I can't say it enough."

Brogue Tesano smiled and shrugged as though he was used to such ravings. "For the chance to take down Marc Ramsey *and* his brother I'd have done the job for nothing."

"Is that right?" Carmen Ramsey's thin arched brows raised a notch and her pen paused over the check she'd been writing.

"But please don't stop your writing." Brogue insisted with a chuckle. "The man's taken a lot Ms. Ramsey." He noted and sobered somewhat.

Carmen continued to write. "The man's dished out a lot. Keep going." She instructed.

Brogue's probing blue stare narrowed. "What's your plan here?" He asked.

Carmen slid the check across the gleaming cherry wood desk and stood. "My plan is simple. I want my brother's life to pass very slowly in front of his eyes before it ends."

Hi Everyone,

*Hopefully you've enjoyed what I consider to be the most emotional of the Ramsey love matches. Taurus and Nile's story tugged at so many heartstrings, yet they managed to triumph. I hope you delighted in all the revelations, new mysteries and new characters that made appearances in this latest chapter.*

*Next, is the seventh and final installment of the Ramsey series. Never fear, the ones you love will have roles to play in the next portion of the saga featuring the Ramsey cousins Sabella, Sabra and Sybilla.*

*For those of you who've asked what I've meant when I've said that everything goes back to Quest and Mick-now you know. I hope you'll enjoy this rather brief peek at Book Seven: A Lover's Soul.*

*Be Blessed,*
*Love,*
*AlTonya*

*www.lovealtonya.com*
*Become a Member of AlTonya's Yahoo web group: LoveAlTonya*

Quest Ramsey sat parked outside his cousin's seemingly drab, unassuming office building. The key was in the Escalade's ignition but had yet to be turned. He'd sat in silence outside Ramsey Bounty just shy of fifteen minutes. He'd replayed the events of the meeting and words of advice passed on from his three cousins.

None of those words helped. Hell, it was easy for Moses, Taurus and Fernando to offer such advice, Quest thought. He knew they loved his wife as much as he did. But it wasn't the same, of course. Everything inside them wouldn't shatter as they told Michaela she'd been cast aside so that her mother could run off with a monster and raise his child. Everything inside them wouldn't shut down as they watched her-watched her heart shred and her soul be reduced to nothing.

A bit over the top? Quest pondered, studying the rhythm his fingers tapped along the steering wheel. Perhaps it was over the top. Many would think so. After all, Michaela Sellars was a tough as nails beauty. It was one of the million and one things he loved about her. But this…this was different. This was a thing he'd watched her struggle with since he'd known her. All that toughness she'd used to pad her soul diminished like mist when she thought of her mother and the life she'd been forced to live when the woman abandoned her.

Now, he was supposed to give her more ugliness to add to the story. How the hell was he supposed to do that?

*She'll hate you if she finds out and discovers you knew and didn't tell her.*

Quest's lashes drifted close over his deep-set stare and he nodded.

He knew Mick loved him as insanely as he loved her. But would that even be enough to keep her from hating him if he kept quiet?

Besides himself and four others, no one else knew. While County was the wild card, he believed she'd agree that this would devastate Mick far too much. As for his cousins…they'd never dare cross him on this.

What of his lovely wife? Quest pondered and leaned his head back on the rest. Without a challenge to occupy her time she'd dig into her task of finding out every aspect of the story. That is, unless she had another *something else* to occupy her time. Grimacing, he started the ignition and sped from the parking lot.

◆   ◆   ◆

## Near Invernesshire, Scotland

"We could've gone anywhere, you know? We still can." Taurus told his wife while resting his head on her chest.

Nile smiled, raking her fingers through his gorgeous hair. They were sprawled across the tangled bed trying to catch their breath following yet another delicious honeymoon romp.

"As long as you are there anywhere's perfect," she sighed and snuggled into him. "But my first choice would be this incredible place."

Taurus began to drop kisses along Nile's body working his way up her lovely dark frame until they were face to face. "Why does everything you say make me want to kiss you?" he asked and proceeded to ply her with another kiss.

Nile whimpered when he freed her lips. "It's the accent," she explained with a wink.

"Must be," Taurus agreed and leaned down to help himself to another taste of her.

Nile eagerly participated thrusting her tongue as languidly as she moved against him. "Nooo," she moaned when he pulled back.

Taurus wouldn't oblige. "Now that we've discussed the fact that this place is perfect, why don't you tell me what's wrong? Is it your parents? The truth," He added quickly spotting the uncertainty in her dark eyes.

Nile's gaze had indeed clouded over. The unease surging through her was an emotion she'd not felt since before she told Taurus the truth about her father.

"I'd like to know," he whispered, his long brows drawing close as he grew more concerned by her silence. "What is it? Now," he insisted cupping her cheek to keep her from looking away.

"I…um…my mother wanted to leave when she found out what my father was really into." She blurted when he gave her chin a warning squeeze. "Cufi Muhammad was a master manipulator though. He-he could think up the best stories, the best…*reasons* to explain how what he was doing was… okay-not harmful."

Taurus closed his eyes regretting then that he made her speak of it. "Baby shhh…" he soothed, kissing her forehead. "You don't have to-"

"No-no you see um…his talent for reasoning was how he got all those girls to come with him." Nile went on, holding onto the sheet as she scooted up in bed. "That's how he got most of them to become part of his disgusting lifestyle. He pacified himself with the thought that those girls were there because they wanted to be-because they'd been rescued from horrible lives, taken from people who didn't understand them."

Taurus couldn't help but think of Jahzara Frazier.

Nile read his thoughts without having to ask for confirmation.

"She'd been through a lot before she was...taken. When Zara killed herself, I couldn't help but wonder."

Nile reached out to stroke his cheek. "About what?"

Taurus rested back on the pillows. "If her being rescued and coming back here was worth it or if she regretted the day we found her."

"What my father was...the things he'd done...I never believed my mother was fully on board with any of it." Nile confessed and turned over in bed to stare at the flames licking the hearth.

Taurus stifled his grimace. The last thing he wanted was his wife pitying a woman who did more than help a monster peddle and destroy young girls. Yvonne Wilson had destroyed her eight year old daughter's life with no help from Cufi Muhammad. Tugging on the sheet, he pulled Nile against him.

"Why are you doing this to yourself, hmm?" He asked, trailing his fingers along her brow.

Nile bit her lip and debated only a second. "I know you won't approve..."

"What?" He prompted when she quieted.

"I want to help her. I want to help my mother-provide counsel, something...it may sound strange to you but I owe her." Nile kept her eyes on the embroidery lining the edge of the top sheet. "She's saved my life three times already-at six when she came to be my new mother, at eighteen when she sent me to California and then just weeks ago when my father tried to kill me."

Taurus nodded. How could he fault her for that? If anything, he loved her even more for wanting to offer her support. "We'll get her the best." He promised and pulled his wife into a hug.

◆　　◆　　◆

The phone rang just as Contessa was heading into the shower to join her fiancé. Recognizing the name on the faceplate, County glanced across her shoulder before answering. "Alan," she almost whispered greeting Alan Claude head of Contessa House's shipping department.

"Hello Contessa, hope this isn't a bad time to call?"

"No uh, no Alan," County glanced across her shoulder once again. "It's not a bad time at all."

"Well you wanted to be contacted when the books arrived from the printer."

"You've got them?"

"Yep. 'Royal Ramsey' hot off the presses and ready to go."

County clenched her hand in a triumphant fist but managed to keep too much glee out of her voice when she addressed her shipping manager.

"I want you to contact Jenean Rays in the fact-checking department. She'll know where to go from there."

"Alright," Alan said while jotting down Jenean's name, "and will she call Spivey or should I-"

"Listen Alan, Spivey Freeman is not to be notified on this do you understand?"

"Well yes, but-"

"Alan if I find out Spivey was contacted-that he's got any idea those books are there-the next thing delivered to the shipping department will be your pink slip."

Alan cleared his throat in recognition of the threat. "It'll be handled just like you asked." He promised, stifling any and all interest in why the publisher was cutting her senior editor out of the loop.

"Good. Thanks Alan, I'll be in touch." County said and set the cordless back to its set. She'd delved into a few moments of deep thought when she was tugged back against a massive frame.

"Thought we were gonna shower together?" Fernando growled deep into her shoulder.

County hooked an arm about his neck. "Well if that's all, then no," she purred.

Fernando chuckled. Effortlessly, he lifted her across his shoulder and carried her into the waiting shower.

♦    ♦    ♦

"Idiots!" Mick hissed while slamming down the phone on her desk.

Quest was walking in just then and witnessed the outburst. "Problems?" he teased, spotting the bridal magazines covering the office. It didn't take many guesses to figure the wedding of the year was the topic of the ill-fated phone call.

"Stupid flower people," Mick grumbled and stabbed a pad with the ball-point of her pen. "How the hell do I know what flowers compliment the *theme* of the wedding?"

"Ah come on, everyone knows how to figure that out."

Mick didn't bother to spare her husband a glance. "Bite me," she suggested dryly in response to his tease. "I don't know why County chose me for this mess. Why can't she and Fernando have a quiet wedding like everybody else?" she wondered while flopping back against her desk chair.

Quest grinned and offered a flip one-shoulder shrug. "Because she's Contessa Warren?" he tried.

Mick sent him an airy salute in agreement. "And I just *had* to be her best friend. I knew there was a catch. So glad I insisted she pick out her own damn dress."

Quest wouldn't dare celebrate before his wife. Still, County's pre-marital requirements offered Mick much needed time-consuming duties in his opinion. Of course, Quest knew his wife. In spite of all the duties involved with the planning of an elaborate wedding, they wouldn't keep Mick preoccupied enough for his liking. *Especially if she's doing the bulk of it in Seattle*, he acknowledged silently.